THEIR COUNTESS

THEIRS
BOOK THREE

JESS MICHAELS

This book is for all the readers who fell in love with this series as much as I did when I wrote it! Look for more coming next year! You guys made my "comeback" so amazing!

And for Michael, my heart. I'm so proud of everything you are.

CHAPTER 1

London

Hux

Peregrine Huxley had always been able to talk himself out of...or into...trouble. Hux had known it from the time he was eight years old, dodging the stomping boots and swinging knives in the kitchen where his mother had worked as a cook. Dodging the crushing fists of his stepfather, too.

He'd known it the first time he'd stolen some bauble...and the first time he'd been caught in the act and had been able to keep himself from gaol through distracting the victim and the investigator and ultimately slipping from their grasp. It had been terrifying, but thrilling.

Over the years, it had become his greatest entertainment to use his charm to entice and trick the fops and their ladies, to slip their jewels and their blunt from their pockets. To make them think he was more or less than he truly was and then take advantage of their foolishness. Just as he was right this moment as he stared across the busy ballroom where he and his partner in crime had gained entry under false names and falser pretenses.

It was a glittering affair, filled with titled and landed gentry of rank and privilege. He didn't belong here, and if any of them looked at him for more than a moment, they might have noticed that. But they never did, so Hux danced and laughed and drank their watered-down punch just as if he belonged.

What a fucking feeling.

He sighed at last and sought out his partner in the crush. He found her surrounded by a circle of rich and handsome men. He couldn't blame them, of course. Zara Cooper was stunningly beautiful. He had been with her, first as an associate and then as a lover, for years, but he still lost his breath when he saw her. She had honey-blonde hair that was bound loosely at the nape of her neck, tendrils framing her oval face and highlighting her bright blue eyes. She smiled at her admirers and it was like someone had turned on the sun in the middle of the ballroom.

They had called her the Countess when she had been a celebrated courtesan years ago. When he'd asked her why, she laughed and said it was because for two years she had only been the lover of earls. Not on purpose, but an accident of fate. But purposeful or not, the nickname fit. Unlike him, she looked like she belonged here. She moved with grace and certainty. She knew how to bat her eyes and turn her head and wrap any man around her finger. She looked like she was a lady of a manor.

She glanced across the room and found his stare. There was a knowing sensuality to the way her gaze flitted up and down his frame. God, but that woman did know how to make him dance to whatever tune she played.

She smiled ever so slightly and then she inclined her head a touch toward one of the gentlemen at her side. The flutter of her fingers was their sign, a beckoning for Hux to come and claim a prize.

He moved through the crowd, always watching, always aware of every threat and opportunity in his surroundings. The men were drifting away from her now, looks of disappointment on their faces that she had given all her attention to the moon-faced gentleman who remained. She moved a little closer to her prey, holding his gaze so that he didn't even notice when Hux took a subtle place behind him.

"Absolutely, sir," she purred. "That does sound like a *great* pleasure. And how fast does a rig like that move, when you really let the horses go?"

Her mark gulped at the seduction of her tone and stammered out some answer. As he did so, Hux carefully slipped his hand into the man's pocket and drew out a jewel-encrusted pocket watch that he palmed as he strolled away with just a quick glance over his shoulder.

Zara winked at Hux. He arched a brow back and her cheeks flamed. They had done quite nicely at this event. Now it was time to have even more fun. He couldn't wait. When it came to Zara, he never could. Never would.

Never wanted to.

~

Zara

Zara moved through the dim hallways of the huge manse where she and Hux had played their games during the ball. She was just behind him, watching him move with an elegance that made his big, wonderfully made form even more interesting. He was a man of so many faces, and she had seen them all. She had never seen even one that made her want to turn away. And so she stayed, both as his partner in their criminal endeavors, and in his bed.

She shivered as she thought of his hands on her, his brown eyes locked with hers as he shattered her over and over again. It never got old. She never wanted him less, which she knew from a vast wealth of experience was a remarkable thing.

He slipped into a parlor and she followed him in. He allowed her to pass him and then caught her arm, using their combined weight to press her back against the flat of the door. He locked the door with one hand and held her there for a moment, his mouth coming down to cover hers. She wrapped her arms around his neck, reveling in the weight of him against her, the control he so rarely took and that she craved. Hux made a soft sound deep in his throat, a rumble that vibrated through her whole body and made her weak down to her trembling knees.

"You taste like their punch," he said, breaking the kiss at last but not moving back as he stared down at her in the fading firelight of the room.

She smiled. "Is that good or bad?"

"Hmmph," he murmured as he buried his mouth against her throat. "I'll tell you once I taste the rest of you."

She laughed even as she dug her fingers into the thick curls of his dark hair, which was peppered with gray and had been since he'd been a very young man. She had always loved that unruly hair, even if they struggled to tame it when he needed to fit into a ballroom. She loved the way it felt when it twisted against her fingers, the way it looked when it rested against her spread thighs or breasts.

"You act like we have all the time in the world," she murmured as he pivoted and backed her toward a settee that faced the fire. "When in reality, it won't be long before *they* start to notice that they're missing their baubles and start trying to recall who didn't belong tonight."

"I like playing dangerously," he said with a chuckle as he sank back into the settee and drew her down into his lap.

That was true. Dangerous games were Hux's specialty. He

always pushed right up the line of where they could be caught...
sometimes just a little beyond. He liked the thrill. She liked the
result when it came to his excitement.

She straddled him, grinding down against the ridge of his cock
that was already begging for her. She couldn't help but moan
softly as he cupped her backside, sliding his hands against her
hips beneath her silk gown. She wanted to feel those warm, rough
hands against her bare skin. Feel them press into her as she
rode him.

"Take it," he whispered, his head tilted back as he watched her.
It was like he could read her mind. Sometimes she thought he
could, at that.

"Show me what you stole first," she demanded even as she
reached between them and slowly unfastened his trousers. She
freed his hard cock and took him in hand, stroking gently as he
reached into his pockets and withdrew tonight's spoils.

He draped a bracelet around the wrist of the hand that held
him so intimately, and she caught her breath at how the sapphires
sparkled in the firelight. Then he took out the pocket watch she
had helped him obtain by distracting the gentleman who had
been rambling to her about horses. She smiled as Hux draped the
chain around her neck and let the heavy watch rest between her
breasts.

"Is that all?" she murmured.

"A few coins," he said, his breath becoming shaky as the strokes
of her hand increased in speed and pressure. "Cufflinks, but I
wouldn't mar your pretty dress, even to see the diamonds rest on
your skin."

She shivered. "Later."

He nodded. "Right now there is only one spoil I want to take,
Zara."

Her breath was short now as she shifted, bunching her dress
around her hips so he could see she wore nothing beneath.

"Fucking minx," he muttered, his fingers sliding beneath the folded silk and gripping her bare thighs as she lowered herself over his hard cock and took him deep inside in one slick thrust.

And then it was magic, one she had studied for years with this man. She rode him, pressing her forehead to his, their gazes locked, their breath matching as she ground toward her pleasure. They went on like that for a while, not too long due to the danger, but long enough that the edge of release teased.

"I want to feel it, Zara, let me feel it," he whispered, his voice rough.

She began to quake around him, her orgasm mounting with every thrust of her hips. She gasped, digging her fingers against the heavy fabric of Hux's jacket as she dropped her head back and rode the intense waves that wracked her body.

"Hux," she moaned, her breath hitching around his name.

"So pretty," he whispered, lifting his hips hard and fast beneath her. She felt the shift in him now that she'd had her pleasure, the drive in him to find his own. His legs shook beneath her and then he buried his head into her shoulder, groaning low and hungry against her skin, his breath hot and ragged as he pumped into her.

She shivered and slowly eased off him. He was still half-hard, his flesh glittering from the slick remnants of their mutual pleasure. She smiled at him wickedly and then leaned over to lick the sensitive head of his cock, tasting their combined come like the sweetest treat. He rose against her with a cry.

"We definitely don't have time for that," he groaned.

She smiled as she lifted her head. "So much for living dangerously."

He arched a brow. "Oh, if you want more danger, then why don't we see if we can take that signet ring from Lord Evensly that you were eyeing when we came in?"

She leaned in to kiss him, slow and steady, reveling in the smoky flavor of his lips, tinged by a hint of whisky. Then she leaned back and nodded. "Fine. Just one more mark and then we go."

"Your wish is my command," he murmured as they both stood and smoothed themselves back into place. She handed over the jewels he had draped over her so no one within would see them, then they linked arms and slipped from the room.

Slipped back into the heady world where neither of them belonged and no one was the wiser.

CHAPTER 2

Richard

From the moment they had entered the ballroom hours before, Richard Fitzroy had been acutely aware of the gorgeous couple he had just watched fuck on the settee. Not only were both of them stunning, her with her honey hair and bright blue eyes, him with that broad-shouldered confidence and angled jaw that seemed ripe for tracing with a finger—or a tongue—but there was something else.

They didn't belong at this gathering. No one else seemed to have noticed and Richard wasn't in the business of outing anyone. So he'd just watched them. As they separated and paraded around the ballroom, her drawing everyone to her like flies to honey, him fading into the background so he could spring their traps. Richard had watched them come back together from time to time, too, the sexual energy between them so palpable that it made him sweat a little. Made his palms itch with a desire to get closer.

It had been a long time since he'd wanted anyone. Anything. He fucked from time to time, of course. He wasn't a monk. A night at a house of pleasure with a man or a woman...or both...

scratched an itch the same way eating food fed an empty stomach. But it was all rather rote.

This draw to the strangers in the ballroom was different. Powerful. He'd fled it, taking refuge in the quiet of a sitting room only to have the pair intrude, not noticing him slouched in a chair in the darkest corner of the room, nursing a scotch. Not noticing him as they drowned their desire in each other.

And revealed the true nature of their attendance tonight.

They were thieves. Richard supposed he could march back into the ballroom and reveal them. Perhaps others would have done so out of some class loyalty. But he felt little of that. He'd grown up with and around the fools in that ballroom. He knew that on the whole they deserved anything that knocked them down a peg.

He pushed from the chair in the corner of the room, feeling the throb of desire their display had caused easing and the cock-stand that had leapt up, demanding attention, softening. He could go back into the ballroom, at least. He could watch them some more, this time with a different eye.

He strode down the hall, smoothing his jacket and calming his breath as he re-entered the ballroom. He gazed across the room immediately, finding the man. *Hux*, the lady had moaned at the height of her passion.

Hux.

He was tall, very tall, with a wiry frame and broad shoulders. He had to be at least three inches taller than Richard and yet he moved with an untamed grace. Like he owned the room. Owned anyone in the room.

As if he felt Richard's stare on him, he turned and their eyes met. Richard couldn't breathe as those dark eyes held his for a beat, two. Hux had crinkles around them, like he smiled often. He wasn't smiling now. Oh, no, he was looking at Richard like he was something…sweet.

Richard swallowed and let his gaze flit down the other man's body. Now Hux did smile, just a fraction, before he turned away and moved into the crowd. Richard felt a strange sense of disappointment. Not that he had any idea what he'd wanted the man to do otherwise. Come over? And what? Steal *Richard's* pocket watch?

A flicker of idea passed through his mind and then he shook it away. He was addled by this heady desire he felt. That was all. And it was in his best interest to just leave.

But as he turned to do so, he saw the woman of the pair moving toward him, her gaze lit with interest just like Hux's had been. Zara, he thought she'd been called. Zara. A beautiful name. One he could easily imagine himself moaning like Hux had moaned it earlier.

"Good evening, sir," she said as she stepped up beside him.

He arched a brow. That was an error. One that would out her if she wasn't careful. After all, a gently bred lady would not have approached a stranger so boldly. Was her mind slightly addled from passion? Or did she do such a thing on purpose, knowing that her beauty and confidence would seduce most men into forgetting the impropriety?

"Miss," he said softly. They stood for a moment, staring out over the ball together. "I don't think we've met before."

"I would remember," she said with a smile that stopped his heart for a moment. Good God, but she was a lovely creature.

"As would I," he breathed, his voice rough. "I'm Richard Fitzoy. And I know your name is Zara, but nothing else."

Her eyes widened. Oh, she didn't like that he knew her real name. She hadn't meant to reveal it and he could see her calculating how he might have known it. But then she smiled and inclined her head. "You are correct. Zara Cooper. A pleasure."

Had she emphasized the word? He couldn't tell if he'd imagined it or if it was real. He felt like he was a little drunk, standing here beside her. Knowing that her partner was circling, probably watching them as he'd been watching every man she'd stood beside during the night.

And even though he knew all their attention was likely a way to lighten his pockets, he didn't step back. "Are you enjoying the gathering?" he asked.

She nodded. "Indeed. It's been lovely. And you?"

He glanced at her and cleared his throat. "I...I fear I do not have the temperament for such things. I attend almost against my will."

Her brows lifted at the honesty of the statement. He was a bit surprised by it, too. He knew Zara wasn't here for any good purpose and yet he'd told her a truth he generally kept to himself.

"That doesn't sound like much fun," she said softly. Then she leaned a little closer. "You shouldn't do things that don't make you happy, Mr. Fitzroy."

Her breath tickled his ear and Richard's eyes came shut at the warmth of it against the sensitive skin. What he wouldn't give to have her closer. To have her ride him like she'd ridden Hux. To have the other man watch.

Richard gripped his hands at his sides. "I wish it were that easy," he ground out with effort.

Her brow wrinkled, and for a moment her gaze stopped being playful and she tilted her head. "Why isn't it?"

His breath caught as he pondered an answer to that question. "Perhaps I've allowed it to be difficult. Embraced it as what must be."

She nodded slowly. "I do understand that. It's easy to fall into a world of...expectation. But becoming more than what people expect us to be is a worthwhile endeavor."

He blinked as they held a gaze for a long moment. This was an unexpected exchange, considering what he knew about the lady. And yet it felt genuine. It felt like this woman was seeing into his soul, a place he had locked away for many years.

Worse, he liked it. It reminded him that he was alive and more than what his birthright or past insisted he be.

He shifted in discomfort at that heady reaction. "You are here with a gentleman, I think."

She swallowed hard and Richard actually saw the moment when her mask came back down over her expression. When she returned to playful thief with a mark and the real connection they had forged so briefly faded away.

"Yes, Huxley is his name," she said, and glanced toward the crowd as if seeking him in the throng. "A friend."

Richard lifted his brows. He'd had many friends in his life, but none he made love to in a parlor in the middle of a ball. "A friend," he repeated slowly. "Fascinating."

"Is it?" she laughed lightly.

He cleared his throat and made a decision so swift and sudden that he didn't have time to argue it with himself. "I'm having a gathering of my own at my estate just outside of London. Next week. From what I've seen tonight, you and your *friend* would make a fine addition."

She leaned back. "That is a kind offer for a man who just met me."

He shrugged. "I'm an excellent judge of character."

Her eyes danced with humor at the statement. Probably judging *him* a fool, but it didn't matter. "As am I. I will see if my friend is available, but if he is, I see no reason we wouldn't enjoy such a gathering."

"Very good," Richard breathed, his heart racing. "I look forward to it."

She smiled. "As do I. Now if you'll excuse me, I think I see Mr. Huxley now. I'll send word by tomorrow afternoon."

"Very good. I look forward to...entertaining you."

Her eyes widened just a fraction and her gaze slid down the length of his body, drinking him in. Her pupils dilated a fraction and she licked her lips. "As do I. Good evening, Mr. Fitzroy."

Then she turned and slipped away, back to Hux across the room and then out of the ballroom with him, the pair chatting softly as they departed. It was only after they were gone that Richard realized all the coins had been removed from his pockets.

He smiled despite the loss. Oh yes. This invitation he'd made in this state of heightened awareness and arousal was ill advised. But he intended to make it fruitful, as well. He intended to make it something he'd never forget.

CHAPTER 3

Hux

Hux looked down at Zara's head bobbing in his lap in time to the carriage as it rumbled along the road a few days later. The pull of her mouth on his cock, the swirl of her tongue... it was all meant to make him come. And it was working. Heated pleasure streaked up his cock, settled in his balls, made his entire being pulse with the edge of release.

He wanted to dig his fingers into her hair as she sucked him off, wanted to feel her rumble with desire, but he couldn't muss her. They were too close to their destination. The home of Richard Fitzroy, the gentleman who had invited them to his gathering at the ball a few days before.

Zara looked up at him, her blue eyes heavy with pleasure. With need. He caught her under the armpits and lifted, tumbling her into his lap. She gasped as he reversed their positions, shoved up her skirts and speared her with his cock, leaning heavily on the carriage wall as he took her in long, languid strokes.

She came in a gasping burst of breath, her skin flushing and her body gripping him in ripping waves of pleasure. It was everything, it was too much, and he couldn't resist the draw of her any longer. He buried his mouth against her neck, breathing her in as he groaned out her name and came inside of her. For a few moments, they remained that way. She stroked along his back, he peppered kisses against the place where her shoulder met her neck. But eventually she laughed softly and pushed him away.

"I must fix myself before we arrive," she insisted.

He grunted and gave her a playful glare as he moved to the seat across from her and went about tucking himself away, smoothing the passion-wrinkled folds in his clothing.

"I think our handsome Mr. Fitzroy might like you tousled by passion, if the way he looked at you at the ball was any indication," he said.

She arched a brow and stifled a smile. "Perhaps. Though was he looking at me or at you that way, Hux?"

Hux cleared his throat. Of course he knew he had garnered as much attention from Fitzroy as she had. He had a sense for men who were built like him. Well-honed after many years of sweaty passion in places where such behavior was encouraged. Pleasure was pleasure to Hux. He didn't care what form it took. He liked all forms.

"That may remain to be seen," he said. "But I think it would be wise if you and I were to create a game plan. After all, we might have a little fun at this gentleman's gathering, but we're also there for a job, are we not?"

"Most definitely," Zara agreed. "Fitzroy has some treasures to uncover, I'm certain. And who knows who else will be in attendance. We could leave this gathering all the richer."

"And satisfied," Hux said softly.

Zara shifted in her seat and met his eyes. "How far can I go?"

Hux lifted his brows. He made no claim to Zara's actions and never had. That was something he was careful about. After all she'd been through, no one deserved total freedom more than she. And yet she always asked before she played, as if she were truly his. And every time it struck the heart of him that he had tried to lock away for decades.

He cleared his throat. "You need to ask?"

There was a moment when a little pain passed over her features, but she wiped it away. "He is very handsome, as we have established. There may be a great many opportunities that come my way. But you and I are...we're partners, aren't we? Shouldn't I have your approval of whatever course of action I choose to take?"

Hux leaned across the carriage, placing a hand on the seat edge on either side of her. Her pupils dilated when he pressed a little closer, invading her space.

"My little minx, if you can land him...why shouldn't you? Opportunity comes in many forms. And if I can watch? All the better."

He saw her intake of breath, her excitement at the idea. She caught the back of his neck and leaned in, kissing him deeply, passionately. She didn't remove her mouth from his as she murmured, "You do know how to move me, Mr. Huxley."

"I hope so," he whispered back, his breath tickling her lips and making her body flex. "It is one of my greatest pleasures to do so."

She laughed and he bathed in the sound of it, even as he leaned away. The carriage was slowing now, pulling up to a fine stone manor at the top of a hill. Hux looked out the window and nodded. Oh yes, there were treasures to be found at such a place if one were reckless enough. He felt like being reckless.

The carriage stopped and there was hustle and bustle as servants came rushing to greet them and help them down. Hux came first and reached back to take Zara's hand. She winked at him as she stepped down and then swept past him toward the front door. It opened as she made her way and they were greeted by their host.

Hux could hardly breathe as he looked at the man. Richard

Fitzroy was truly handsome, with thick, dark hair, a low brow that always made him look intense and a jaw that could cut glass. There was no doubt he had to garner the attraction of men and women alike. He had dark blue eyes the color of pure sapphires that always seemed to be watching. Even now they flitted over first Zara, then Hux, then back to their carriage, reading, judging, perhaps. What conclusion he came to was impossible to detect. He revealed nothing of it in his expression.

Immediately, Hux felt his hackles rise. A sense of...premonition filled him that he didn't fully understand. He'd been in worse situations over the years, but he felt that thrill up his spine that said...*danger.*

He didn't ignore it, but he didn't allow it to be seen. He kept his expression relaxed, a friendly smile of greeting. Zara continued forward, her hand outstretched.

"Mr. Fitzroy," she purred. "How grand to see you again. And this is a lovely home, I cannot wait to see the rest of it."

Fitzroy offered his own smile as he caught Zara's hand and raised it to his lips, lingering just a moment too long with his mouth on her skin. "Miss Cooper," he said, and let his gaze slide to Hux. "Mr. Huxley. A pleasure to see you both. Please, come in."

He motioned into the foyer and Zara stepped around him. As Hux did the same, he felt keenly aware of the presence of this man. Dominating, sensual, unreadable. His blood was on fire, he was on edge and he liked the feeling.

A perfectly liveried butler took their wraps and then Fitzroy led them to a pretty parlor off the foyer. A pretty, yet strangely quiet and empty parlor. Zara looked at Hux over her shoulder even as she took one of the seats Fitzroy motioned to as he went to the sideboard and began to fix drinks for them all.

Hux stepped behind Zara, resting a hand briefly on her shoulder. "As Miss Cooper said, this is a beautiful home, Mr. Fitzroy."

Fitzroy chuckled before he turned and handed over a sherry

for Zara and a whisky for Hux. "Thank you," he said, sinking into a chair across from Zara. "I like it. How was your journey?"

"The carriage ride was lovely," Hux said, glancing down at Zara. Her cheeks pinkened ever so slightly and he stifled a laugh. Even after all these years and all her experience, he could still make her blush. And it was a triumph every time.

Fitzroy arched a brow. "I imagine you two must have a great many rousing *conversations* in a carriage. A perfect place to truly connect, without any eyes watching."

Hux's brow lowered and he took in Fitzroy. Was he being obtuse or speaking in double meaning? Strange to say, Hux couldn't tell and that was fascinating in and of itself. He could almost always read others. It made this man all the more intriguing, certainly.

Fitzroy settled into a chair across from them. He crossed one leg over the other and leaned back, his drink dangling from his fingertips. "Won't you sit, Mr. Huxley?"

Hux inclined his head and came around the settee to sit beside Zara. He slung an arm along the back of the couch, not touching Zara but insuring she knew his presence was near should she need it. It was a claim, he supposed, and perhaps he made it to test Fitzroy. After all, he was endlessly fascinated by the way the man's blue gaze moved over both of them. Most men like this one weren't so bold.

"To answer your question," Hux said softly. "I suppose Zara and I do have interesting conversations when we are alone. Friends often do."

"It takes a very special friend to have a truly deep conversation though, doesn't it?" Fitzroy pressed, his gaze locking with Hux.

"Yes." Hux didn't elaborate. "You must have a great many *friends*, though."

Fitzroy let out a little snort and turned his face. "And why would you say that? You hardly know me."

"And you hardly know us," Zara interjected as she took a sip of her drink. "And yet here we are. Sometimes the stars align, don't they, and introduce like-minded individuals."

Fitzroy was silent a beat, two and then he nodded. "I think we are like-minded, Miss Cooper. I felt it the first moment I saw you in the ballroom. And I look forward to getting to know you, and Mr. Huxley, during your stay here."

Zara smiled at Fitzroy and Hux watched the spark between them crackle. This was the kind of man she had once seduced and been protected by. The kind of man who would take her to plays and art exhibits rather than use her charms to rob some poor fool of his blunt. The kind of man who could safeguard her in ways that went beyond Hux's means, no matter how many riches he locked away. He shifted slightly as a faint gripped him. It was such a foreign emotion, one he normally didn't allow himself to feel. He didn't like it.

Zara tensed beside him as if she sensed his shift in mood and cleared her throat. "I'm sure we will have a great many opportunities to do just that, Mr. Fitzroy. Though I'm certain you will also be distracted by your other guests. Are we the first to arrive then?"

Fitzroy didn't answer, and the emotions Hux had been allowing to rule over him were pushed aside. There was something...off about this situation. He knew it as well as he knew his own face in the mirror.

"It seems odd that we would be, as Miss Cooper and I are known for our always being fashionably late." He arched a brow. "Did we misunderstand your invitation and somehow make the ghastly mistake of being early?"

Fitzroy's cheek twitched in half a smile. "Neither late nor early, I'm afraid to tell you. On the contrary, you are right on time."

Zara glanced over and Hux and he saw the little flicker of her anxiety. She had noted the strangeness, as well, felt the same concerns that now flooded him. "Then the others must be already in their quarters."

Fitzroy shrugged. "Yes, the quarters. After our drinks, I'll have you taken to yours. But I suppose we must discuss a...*delicate* subject."

Hux tensed further. "And what is that, Mr. Fitzroy?"

"Should I have one room or two prepared?" he asked softly, his gaze moving to Zara. Perhaps he was looking for embarrassment.

Of course, she revealed none. She arched a brow like she owned this man and this room. "One. I think you already guessed that Mr. Huxley and I share a very *special* friendship."

The corners of Fitzroy's mouth tilted and Hux saw no judgment. "Of course." He got to his feet. "Let me tell my people so they may take your things to the right place."

He stepped out, and Zara immediately turned to Hux. "You notice he didn't really answer the question about others coming to join us?"

"Of course," Hux said softly. "He is cagey. Not nervous, though, but clearly hiding something." He stared toward the door. "I don't like it."

"You think he's dangerous?" she asked.

He shrugged. "Every man can be dangerous, as you well know."

"Hmmm." She sipped her drink. "Then I suppose we'll have to suss it out. We're clever."

Hux leaned down and pressed a brief kiss to her lips, hoping to calm her fears a little, even if he still clung to his own discomfort. "It will be a challenge."

As he straightened, Fitzroy re-entered the room, and for a moment his pupils dilated as he looked at them. "Your chamber is ready. I'll allow my butler, Peyton, to take you up, as I have bit of business to attend to in my study for the next hour or so. We'll have tea at three, so you'll have time to rest yourselves before that."

Hux wrinkled his brow. Fitzroy had been all intense interest and flirtation a moment before, but now he was acting just like any normal host. A little detached, friendly but ultimately disinterested. Still, Zara pushed to her feet and set her empty glass aside. She slid her hand into the crook of Hux's arm, her fingers tightening, sending a message to remain collected so they could regroup.

He let out a long breath and then led her from the room. "Of course. We will see you then, Mr. Fitzroy."

Fitzroy inclined his head and Hux felt him watching as they walked down the hall toward the staircase. The butler took them to the chamber, and after a few moments of polite exchange, he left. Hux leaned on the door and stared at Zara once they were alone.

"Something is definitely amiss."

She nodded. "Then perhaps we should do a little snooping. See if we can determine a little more about the handsome Mr. Fitzroy and if he is a threat to us."

He agreed, and they exited the room and moved up the hall. Zara checked doors on one side of the hallway, Hux the other. Most were guest chambers, plain and not telling of anything about the man who owned the estate except that he had no other guests here but them.

But at last they reached a large double door and Hux looked down at her. "The chamber of the man himself, I think."

She nodded. "If he's hiding something, it might be here. And he did say he was going to be in his study for an hour. This is as safe a time as ever."

Hux nodded and checked the door. It was locked, but that was nothing. Zara pulled a slender lock pick from within the pile of curls styled carefully atop her lovely head, and as she stood by, watching for anyone who might interrupt them, Hux worked on granting them entry. When there was the slight sound of the catch giving, he almost let out a moan of pleasure. God, but that was one of the best feelings in the world.

Not *the* best, of course.

He opened the door and peeked inside. When he found it empty, he pushed it wider so that Zara could go first. "My lady," he said, his voice low as she passed with a soft laugh.

They separated instantly. She moved up one side of the room, he the other. It seemed to be a perfectly normal chamber. Fine, yes, oh very fine with its flawlessly pressed linens on the big bed and its tasteful furniture. But Hux had been to dozens of rooms like these in the past, for mischief...and a few times for fun, long before he'd met Zara.

There was nothing special here, nothing that would show why both he and Zara felt such a sense of unease about their host. Hux was about to rejoin Zara across the room, when a small wooden box on top of the dressing table caught his eye. It was beautifully carved, probably worth a fortune by itself. The kind of compartment that usually held very special, very expensive things. He glanced over his shoulder. Zara was at the fireplace, fiddling with the miniatures on its mantel, as if she might reveal a secret chamber.

Of course, once at a house party in Sharpsworth, that had been exactly what they'd found. Crowning moment for them both.

He returned his attention to the box. Carefully he lifted its top and caught his breath. The compartment was lined with dark green velvet and in its folds laid a huge emerald brooch. Hux's mouth watered as he stared at it, drawn to it like a moth to a flame.

It likely wasn't Fitzroy's. Not that Hux hadn't known plenty of men who liked to wear ladies' things. Nothing wrong with it. But Fitzroy didn't seem the type. Did he have a wife? Was *that* the cause for his strange behavior this afternoon?

He wrinkled his brow. Why was he wasting so much time trying to determine the habits of his prey? That wasn't like him. He reached out and caught the brooch, reveling in its weight for a moment. He was about to place the item in his pocket when a door to a side chamber opened and into the room stepped Richard Fitzroy.

"Well, well, well, I thought it would take you at least a day before you made this particular move," he drawled as he leaned against the doorjamb and arched a brow at both of them.

CHAPTER 4

Zara

Despite the dangerous activities she and Hux involved themselves in regularly, it was not a usual occasion to be caught in the act so completely. Zara's heart raced as she ran through a dozen scenarios in her head. Hux had always told her that if they were ever caught, he would take the blame and the punishment. He had refused to listen when she tried to argue, and she knew he would continue to do so if they were accused of theft. Which meant he would take the entire weight of what could be thrust upon them by this man.

Transportation. Hanging.

Her heart raced and she lunged forward to make some excuse. To explain somehow and protect him, but stopped when Hux sent a warning glance her way.

"Mr. Fitzroy," Hux said, with all the appearance of calm that she knew he could not be feeling. "What a delight."

"Indeed," Fitzroy said with just as much calm. "First my coins at the ball last week," He glanced toward Zara with a small smile.

"Well done, by the way, I didn't even feel you take them. What a disappointment."

Zara swallowed hard. "I don't know what you're talking about."

Fitzroy chuckled. "Of course not. But I think you won't be able to find an excuse for this. That was my late wife's, you know. I bought it for her on the occasion of our first anniversary what feels like a lifetime ago."

Hux's jaw tightened, then he reached behind him and carefully set the emerald back into the case where he'd apparently found it. He closed the lid with a light thud and inclined his head. "There you have it. No harm done."

Fitzroy arched a brow. "Does that normally work?"

"Talking myself out of situations? You'd be surprised." Hux said just as evenly. "I will continue to do so if you tell me what you intend to do now."

"You'd hit me, wouldn't you? Send me to the floor next to my bed and run, except for her." Fitzroy nudged his head toward Zara, and she caught her breath. Of course he was correct. Hux had boxed for a while in the underground and been quite good at it. Without her to worry about, he could certainly fight his way out of this situation. But he'd never leave her behind.

"Hux—"

Hux lifted a hand toward her without looking away from Fitzroy. "No."

For a long moment the two men simply stared at each other. Then, to Zara's surprise, Fitzroy shrugged. "I would like to have a reasonable discussion with you two and come up with some reasonable solutions to the problem that has been created here today. Can we agree to that?"

Hux's jaw twitched, but he jerked out a slight nod. "Yes."

Fitzroy looked toward her. "Zara?"

"Yes," she breathed, and hated how her voice shook. Both the men were so calm, but she couldn't be. Not when stark terror on behalf of Hux rushed through her. They always danced on the knife's edge of consequences and usually were both clever enough to keep themselves from falling. But today they had been sloppy. Why? Was it because neither of them fully understood the situation they had walked into? Was it because they each found Fitzroy so attractive that they had miscalculated?

Or were they just getting careless because it had been a long time since they'd come close to the very real dangers that their behaviors could create. Too full of their own success to see the danger coming until it was too late.

Her heart leapt and she stepped forward. "Please," she whispered. "I will do anything."

Hux shook his head slightly and Fitzroy's eyebrows both lifted at her entreaty. He didn't answer, though, but motioned Hux over to the chairs by the fire. Slowly, Hux followed the silent order, even as he motioned for Zara to stay by the door where she stood. Did he intend to create situation where *she* could run? Of course he would. The man would sacrifice himself for her.

She knew it in her bones.

Fitzroy waited until Hux had sat and then stepped to the wooden box. He opened it and stared at the emerald within, his gaze unreadable but for a slightly tightening of his lips. He looked toward Zara. It seemed they were negotiating now—for Hux's life?

"This is an expensive piece." He lifted it and showed her, as if he knew she hadn't had a good look at it before. Like he'd been watching them all along. Her heart raced faster. "Do you need the money?"

From his seat before the fire, Hux snorted out a harsh laugh. "Just like a toff not to understand that everyone bloody well needs money."

Zara jerked her gaze to him. Hux was generally cool and collected in all situations. This hard edge was not something he often unleashed. Certainly not toward her. But he would always rather lure flies with honey. It seemed he feared for what would happen next as much as she did.

Fitzroy gave a soft smile, as if the snapping remark did not offend. "You two treat this as a game," he said. "It's fascinating. There is an energy to it that clearly gives you both a thrill despite the obvious dangers. So I am asking you, Zara: do you do what you do for money or for fun?"

Hux shifted in the chair, his knuckles whitening against the arms. Zara rushed forward, almost as if she could place herself between them as a buffer, and pressed a hand to his shoulder, holding him in place even though she knew he could shrug her off if he chose to do so.

"Both," she burst out, locking her eyes with Fitzroy's and marveling, even in the midst of this terrible situation, at how very blue they were.

"What else do you do for fun?" Fitzroy asked softly, the innuendo hanging in the air. He then looked past her, holding his gaze on Hux. She felt the crackle of awareness hanging in the air between the two men, as much as she felt it between herself and their captor. Despite the danger.

"What do you mean?" she asked, even though she knew. She wanted him to spell it out, almost to see if he would dare.

Fitzroy tilted his head. "You pretend not to know? Why do you think I invited you here, Zara?"

She blinked. "I-I'm not sure. We thought we were coming to hunt, but it's clear you are the hunter. Clear you wanted us to do something that would put us under your power."

For a moment a look of pure horror crossed Fitzroy's face and then he slowly shook his head. "I don't care about the brooch, Zara." He tossed the emerald toward Hux and he reached up one hand to catch it, even as he stared in confusion at Fitzroy. "I have no intention of calling the authorities and reporting this. Nor of reporting what happened at the ball. If you come *under* me in any way, it won't be because you were forced to do so."

"What the fuck are you about?" Hux growled.

"I invited you here because I was intrigued by you at the ball. By the way you two so effortlessly controlled a place where you so clearly did not belong. And by that energy between you that I described earlier. There was such life to it and I have not felt entirely connected to life in a very long time. I invited you here because I want you."

"No," Hux breathed.

Zara jumped at the tone and glanced at him. There he was, scooted to the edge of the chair, coiled like he would lose control at any moment. Her partner, her lover, her...her everything, even though she never dared say it, even after all this time. Even though Fitzroy was claiming he wasn't going to bring them to harm, it was clear Hux didn't believe him. He still thought this was an attempt at coercion.

And perhaps he was right, but when Zara stared into Fitzroy's eyes, she didn't see threat. Or at least not the kind Hux feared and would sacrifice everything to protect her from.

"Whether or not you tried to steal something from me, whether or not I caught you, I always intended to make a very specific type of proposal. Perhaps the most indecent one I've ever made, but also the most tempting."

"No!" Hux snapped again, and now he was on his feet. He rushed past Zara and right into Fitzroy's space. Fitzroy didn't move, even when their chests touched. He merely looked up into Hux's face with an almost impassive expression.

Almost. Zara saw the flare of heat in the other man's eyes and it didn't seem to be anger or aggression. Still, the good will of a gentleman could quickly shift to ill intent, she knew that better than most. She stepped up next to Hux and took his hand.

"Hux," she said softly. "Look at me."

He glared hard at Richard and then slowly shifted his gaze to Zara. His expression softened. Became pained. "Zara—"

She shook her head. "Stop. Please."

He didn't finish whatever he would say, but she still saw his worry. "You don't do this anymore," he said after a long pause. "Not this way."

"I believe him when he says he isn't trying to use this against me," she said. "You are trying to protect me, as you always protect me. But I want to know what Mr. Fitzroy is offering before I decide what is in my own best interest."

"You think a man like this cares about your best interest? He claims he won't harm you, harm us, but you know better than to trust—"

"Yes," she interrupted. "I know better. So you can trust me to be intelligent. Can't you?"

He held her stare for a long moment and then shook her head. "Don't make some bargain to save me when it turns out this fop is a liar, Zara. I'm not bloody worth it."

He turned them and left the room. Left her alone with a man who now knew at least some of her secrets. Whether he could truly be trusted with them was another story entirely.

Richard

The way Zara bent her head, her breath coming in harsh heaves, Richard wondered if he'd gone too far. Had he thought the brooch might be a trap for them? Certainly. After all, he knew they were thieves. He wanted to see when and how they'd make a move because they were so bloody interesting to him. However, the fact that he'd caught them was now so tangled up with the proposal he'd hoped to make to the pair about becoming his lovers was unfortunate, indeed.

He couldn't blame Hux for not believing his motives, even if Richard knew they were true. Why would someone streetwise and certain like Huxley have any trust for a, as he had so eloquently put it…a *fop*? Richard knew full well that men of his ilk were often untrustworthy and used their privilege to destroy and coerce and harm.

He would have to be very careful in how he proceeded.

"He is fiery," he said as mildly as he could manage when his own heart was throbbing with anticipation.

She stared off at the door where Huxley had stormed a moment before. "He is…protective," she corrected.

"Jealous?" Richard asked.

"No," she laughed, a low, husky sound that heated Richard's blood. "He isn't jealous. Not how you mean."

"Then how?"

She walked away, pacing to the window where she stared down into the garden behind Richard's home. When she was quiet for what felt like an eternity, he took a step toward her. "You owe me nothing. I'm a stranger."

She glanced over her shoulder. He thought she must know how alluring she looked when she did it. "A stranger who is offering me money… in exchange for bedding me. That is what we're talking about, isn't it, when you use the term *indecent proposal?*"

Now it was his turn to be silent, as much as he wished to say more. To ask for more. To touch her.

"If Huxley believes I'm threatened…forced…" she murmured at last, and then trailed off with a shiver.

Richard cleared his throat. "Yes, I saw the results. It's quite intoxicating in its way."

"You think so?" she asked, facing him fully now, arms folded.

He nodded. "He's a fascinating man. His connection to you is no less intriguing than anything else about him."

She shifted ever so slightly but didn't answer. So she was as protective of Hux as he was of her. Richard let out a long breath. "Let me ask you this, Zara: are you interested in my proposition? Without worrying about his reaction if it isn't jealousy. If I had approached you in a different way and offered you a significant payment for…say…a week of your time…"

"A week," she murmured.

"I think a man might need a week to really enjoy time with you, Zara."

She shivered, an almost imperceptible movement, but one that emboldened Richard. He held his breath as he let her take her time to answer.

"How much is significant?" she asked at last.

Richard laughed at the question, but swept out a small notebook and charcoal pencil he often carried in his inside pocket. He wrote down a figure and handed over the sheet.

Her eyes bulged. "Did you add one too many zeros to this number, Mr. Fitzroy?" she asked.

He smiled. "No. That is the figure I'm offering."

"That and your silence about whatever you saw at the party last week and whatever you discovered in your chamber today," she said.

He shook his head. "My silence is not for sale. I offer it freely, as I said. If you refuse the money, refuse the proposal of pleasure together, I will send you on your way, with my silence insured."

"And how am I to trust that statement?" she asked.

He shrugged. "I suppose you would have to see if I uphold my promise. But my word is my bond. I know that I won't go back on it and I know you will see that is true, as well."

"So it is only my body you are paying for."

"I hope that it won't only be yours," he said, and glanced toward the door. "But I clearly need to negotiate with the other party in a different way."

"And what if he says no."

"Then the offer stands for only your lovely company," he said. She stared at the paper again, tracing her finger over the amount he had written. He cleared his throat. "So now that the boring bits are resolved, I ask again: do you want what I'm offering, Zara?"

She swallowed hard and let her gaze flit up and down the length of his body in a slow sweep. The corners of her lips quirked up as she did so and her gaze grew a little more heavy.

"I admit, I do, Mr. Fitzroy," she said at last.

And even though this was just a lark, a game, Richard felt a swell of relief at the answer. He leaned forward. "Richard. I think for what is about to happen, it would be better if you called me Richard."

"Richard," she repeated softly.

The sound of his name coming from her lips made a great shiver work through his entire body. There were very few times when a man was called by his given name in Society. It had been a long time since he heard a lady use it.

His voice was rough as he said, "Why don't you let me speak to Huxley? Let him know I'm not a threat to you as he clearly fears."

She shook her head swiftly. "I don't know—" she began.

He leaned in and let his fingers trace the soft curve of her cheek. Her breath caught at the motion and her words ceased instantly.

"I can be...persuasive," he insisted.

She held his gaze for a long moment and then nodded. "Very well. You seem the kind of man who could not be deterred, at any rate."

"Not when I want something," he conceded. "I will prove that to you. Very soon." He stepped away with great difficulty. "Why don't you return to your chamber and I'll send for you when it is done?"

She still seemed ill at ease with the idea, but she sighed as she walked to his door. "Very well."

When she was gone, Richard smoothed his jacket and looked toward his bed. Soon enough he would have what he wanted. At least partly. And now it was time to make sure he got everything he desired...and perhaps a little more.

CHAPTER 5

Hux

Hux stood at the window at one of Fitzroy's many parlors, staring down at the garden below as he flexed his hands in and out of fists at his sides. His heart and mind were racing and he could not stop the tide of his wild reactions.

He thought of Zara. Thought of the desperation on her face a short time ago. He'd spent the last few years working hard to keep that look from her face. Now it was there because of him. Because he'd been reckless, played a game...lost for both of them.

The door behind him opened and he looked over his shoulder to watch Fitzroy entering the room. He leaned back against the door after he shut it and just looked at Hux for a long, charged moment. Hux wasn't certain if he wanted to punch the man in the face...or do something far more pleasurable. Perhaps both.

"You want to protect her," Fitzroy said at last.

Hux shook his head. "What would you know about it."

"I'm not blind," Fitzroy said. "And my offer is something that troubles you."

"I don't want her cheapened," Hux said, turning back to the

window even though he was very aware of every move the other man made. He *felt* him come closer and Hux's breath hitched.

And then it ceased as Fitzroy's arms came around him on either side. He rested his hands on Hux's stomach, fingers bunching there against the muscle. His pelvis brushed Hux's backside and Hux felt the hard length of him there, pressing in the most intoxicating way. He couldn't help himself…he leaned into the other man's broad chest with a sharp exhalation.

"I promise you," Fitzroy said, breath hot against his neck, arousing beyond measure, "that my request wasn't about cheapening her."

Hux let out a long breath. "You aren't blackmailing her into fucking you?"

"No. Never." There was something so certain about his words and his tones. Something that made Hux want to…*believe* him. "It's about pleasure, Huxley. I want her." There was a pause that seemed to last a lifetime and then Fitzroy added, "And I want *you.*"

Hux's knees felt weak. He gripped his hands against the windowsill as if he could gain purchase there. But there was nothing solid about the world anymore. He was washing out on erotic seas, and the man behind him was the siren drawing him farther from shore.

"Join us," Fitzroy continued, his mouth hot on Hux's ear now, his tongue darting out to trace the shape of it. "To protect her if you feel you need to. And for our mutual pleasure."

Hux didn't answer as he continued to stare out the window. If he did this, he would get to feel even more of this man's touch. And he would also be on guard, perhaps in a way Zara wouldn't, if Fitzroy suddenly decided to turn his "offer" against them.

Hux finally got up the strength to turn around, turn to the man who had him pinned against the glass. He dragged his fingers into Fitzroy's hair and then their mouths met. There was nothing gentle about the kiss, nothing exploratory. It was all heat, all sloppy, reckless passion. Fitzroy drove his tongue, mimicking some rhythm he wanted to make with his cock, and Hux found his hips jolting forward with each thrust like he was already being taken.

At last he broke away, his gaze locked with the other man's. "I think you know my answer," he panted, and watched as Fitzroy's lips quirked in a small, cocksure smile. "But she has to agree. Do you agree, Zara?"

He asked the question without looking at the door. He already knew she was there. He always knew when she was there, no matter what he was doing or with whom.

Fitzroy turned, and finally Hux found the ability to stop focusing on him. They both looked at the door. Zara was standing just inside, beautiful as always. God, she was beautiful. It always shocked Hux, no matter how many times he looked at her. Right now her face was flushed and her hands trembled at her sides.

"You know me too well not to know what I want, Hux," she said, her voice shaking like her body. "And I know you just as well. I knew from the moment you looked at Richard how much you want to touch him. Touch us."

Richard. She'd said Fitzroy's given name and now Hux wanted to hear her moan it. *He* wanted to moan it.

"Then come here," Hux managed to choke out.

She moved then, staggering steps across the room. Richard held out a hand to her, allowing him to draw her into the circle of both men. She lifted her mouth to Hux first and he took it, reveling in her as he always did, no matter how many times he'd felt those lips against his. He had never tired of her taste and he never would.

He sucked her tongue lightly and she made a little moan before she broke the contact. He slowly turned her toward Fitzroy and she smiled as she wrapped her arms around his neck. Hux watched as the other man leaned into her, careful, slow, exploratory as he first brushed his lips to hers and then fully kissed her.

Richard's tongue made long, slow strokes against Zara's, and Hux felt her go weak. He stepped closer, rocking his body against her from behind even as he shored her up with his weight at her back.

She reached up, cupping Hux's chin with her hand, stoking against the persistent whiskers there as she continued to kiss Richard. Then she drew him down, into their space. Suddenly they were all kissing, tongues and breath merging in a heated frenzy. Hux cupped Richard's face with one hand and slid his fingers between their bodies to stroke Zara's nipple through the silk of her gown. She made a soft, barely human sound of pleasure and threw her head back, breaking the kiss at last.

Richard's pupils were so dilated his eyes were almost black, and his voice was strained as he said, "Let's take this back to my bedchamber, shall we?"

No one answered. They all just started moving, hands still gripping and sliding against each other even as they staggered back toward the bedchamber. The door had been left open, so they all filed in. Immediately, Richard tugged Zara to him, kissing her even more deeply than he had before. Hux shut the door, pressing his hand against it after he'd turned the key, bracing himself as he watched the woman he'd called lover for years drown in a man he both wanted and couldn't fully trust.

And all he could think about was how much he wanted to lose himself in both of them. How much he wanted to surrender fully to the pleasure they were about to exchange. He just hoped he could.

Zara

Zara couldn't breathe. No just because Richard's mouth was locked against hers, his kisses becoming more commanding, more forceful with every expert swipe of his tongue. She was beginning to feel weightless, dizzy with this man's attentions and with the knowledge of what was about to transpire between all three of them.

He broke the kiss, panting down at her with a look of almost... confusion in his eyes. About what, she couldn't say. This was what they'd all agreed to, after all.

She trembled as she turned away and looked at Hux. He was standing frozen at the door, his hand gripped in a fist against the surface, just staring at the two of them.

"I want you," she murmured, crooking her finger and knowing he would come. Hux always came when she called. And when he did so with that heated look of desire on his face...well, it was everything she'd ever wanted and more.

"Then you shall have me," he said as he reached her, cupping her cheeks so gently as his mouth came down on hers. His tongue probed past her lips, tasting her, tasting Richard by default, and he let out a shuddering moan that made her thighs clench. Moving him had always been one of her greatest triumphs.

He stepped back and turned her around, unfastening her dress in a few expert flicks of his fingers. She watched Richard as he did so, holding his gaze boldly, judging every reaction as Hux finally slid his rough fingers to lift the soft fabric off her shoulders and the gown drooped around her waist, leaving her bared from there up.

"No undergarments," Richard murmured.

"Never wears them," Hux said, pushing her hair aside and lightly nibbling along the sensitive skin of her neck. "It makes life ever so much more fun."

"I would say so," Richard said as he reached out and cupped Zara's breasts gently. He gasped as his fingers closed around the softness, as he rubbed a thumb back and forth against the hard nipple.

Electric pleasure rushed through Zara and she arched, pressing her head into Hux's shoulder, feeling his fingers tighten against her arms as he offered her up to this other man and his sure touch.

"She tastes like a dream," he murmured, his voice hypnotic.

Richard made a rumbling sound deep from his chest and bent, lifting Zara's breast slightly and swirling his tongue around the hard tip. He sucked, first softly, then harder, and Zara cried out as she dug her fingers into his hair and held him against her body.

Hux was breathing heavily behind her now. She felt the ridge of his cock hardening against her backside and her mouth began to water for it.

"Shall I take the rest off?" Hux asked. "And show you what really makes her scream?"

Richard released her nipple with a wet pop. "I'd like that."

He let his hands slide down over her abdomen. Together the men looped their fingers into the folded remainder of her gown and pushed, gliding it over her hips until she stood in only pretty stockings and slippers.

Hux went down on his knees behind her, dragging his mouth along her spine and over her backside as he did so. She jolted at the wet, hot path he had created, resting her hands on Richard's shoulders to keep herself from falling over thanks to shaking knees and blurring vision.

Hux was licking and nipping her thighs, pressing his fingers against the pretty garters tied to hold her stockings up. "Should I leave them on or take them off?"

Zara looked down, expecting that he was asking her. But she realized as she did so that he was looking at Richard. And Richard was staring back, mouth a little slack, as if he was stunned.

"Leave them," Richard finally ground out, his voice rough and low and dangerous.

Hux smiled. "A man after my own heart. There is something about having her legs wrapped around your waist and feeling that silk brush your skin."

Zara shivered. "You needn't talk about me like I'm not here," she managed to choke out.

Hux laughed as he let the flat of his hand smooth up her thigh, just tease between her legs. "I assure you, sweet, all we can see is you."

She almost laughed. "I don't think that's true. You two see each other just as plainly. And it drives me wild."

"We haven't even begun to drive you wild," Richard assured her. "Will you move to the bed?"

Hux released her and rocked back on his heels as he watched her move to the bed. She climbed up and rested back on the pillows, carefully opening her legs and arranging herself for the best view for them both. Hux stood and together the men stood staring at her.

Richard licked his lips. "I want a taste. Show me."

Hux braced his hands on the edge of the bed and smiled up at Zara with an expression of erotic promise that made her heart studder. "Oh, with great pleasure."

He moved up on the mattress and positioned himself between her legs, opening her wider. "So pretty," he all but purred as he stroked a finger through the wet evidence of how aroused she already was.

He lifted it for Richard to see, and Zara gasped as Richard leaned forward and sucked the finger into his mouth, swirling his tongue around and around as Hux let out a moan.

"You do have a talented tongue," Hux whispered harshly, then winked down at Zara. "Are you ready to feel it? To have us both taste you until you are shaking?"

"Please," she all but sobbed. "Please."

He flashed a half-grin and then lowered his head between her legs. His curly hair settled against her thighs, and she cried out as he gave one languid lick along the full length of her pussy. She lifted into him, clenching at the coverlet as every sensation in her trembling body spiraled into intense focus on the heated place between her legs and Hux's tongue as he stroked over her again and again and again.

He was building her pleasure, maneuvering her with ease toward leg-shaking release. After so many years together, he could do it almost effortlessly. Better yet, he seemed to revel in the act, revel in watching her body bend and shake and convulse in the pleasure his mouth gave. Never was he harder than after a languid afternoon of his tongue on her...in her.

"I see," Richard said softly, moving toward the bed at last. He cupped her cheeks and kissed her, deep and slow. Hux's mouth faltered on her, and she glanced down to find him watching them kiss even as he continued to lick and please.

"Look at me," Richard ordered, and she did so, locking her gaze with his ridiculously blue one and losing herself in the intensity of his stare, along with the powerful pleasure of Hux's tongue. "Don't come, Zara. No matter how much he pleases you, you can't come yet. Not until I tell you."

She moaned at the idea that she would hand over the permission of her pleasure to another person. Hux had never claimed that. He gave freely, often without asking for anything in return. But the idea that this tall, handsome man...almost a stranger... would hold the keys to when she quaked was...intoxicating.

"May I beg?" she gasped, twisting as Hux began to suck her clitoris, tormenting her.

Richard leaned in, caging her head with his hands, letting his lips just brush over hers as he whispered, "I demand that you do. Do you hear me? I *demand* it, Zara. Beg him. Beg me. Tell me every filthy thing you'll do if I allow your release. Tell me every moment of what being poised on the edge does to you. Give it all to me and perhaps I'll set you free to scream this house down. But do not come until I give permission."

She nodded, a jerky motion she barely controlled because Hux's tongue was moving faster now and she was already on the edge that Richard would deny. She lifted her head to kiss him again, looking for distraction, but he only laughed, and when he bent his mouth to her, it was against her throat.

He dragged his tongue down over her breasts, swirling around first one nipple, then the other. Tugging there, matching his rhythm to Hux's as she writhed.

"Beg," he repeated, this time sharply.

"Please!" she cried out, thrashing her head on the pillows and lifting her hips helplessly. "Please let me come for him. I want to come."

"What else do you want?" Richard encouraged as his mouth drew down over the soft swell of her stomach.

He was almost between her legs now, almost to where Hux continued to torment her, sucking and licking, swirling his tongue and then spearing her with it. Building her toward the edge and then denying it by altering his rhythm. Whatever game they were playing, he was fully invested. His gaze glittered as he looked up at her, pupils dilated with her torment.

"I want you both to lick me," she gasped. "I want you to put your fingers in me. I don't want to be able to tell who is touching me. I just want to feel you both."

Richard chuckled against her hips even as he settled a hand on Hux's back. Hux moaned against her skin and the vibration nearly set her off. She groaned and twisted, trying to get closer, trying to move farther away. Anything just to ease the ache that was building so high inside of her that she feared she would shatter when she was finally allowed to fall.

She forced her gaze open, made herself watch as Richard nudged Hux to the side, widening her legs even farther so that one thigh was draped over each of their shoulders. The stretch was lewd and delicious, and she lifted toward them as Richard bent his head. Hux turned toward him, and for a moment their tongues tangled against her sensitive clitoris.

"Oh God," she gasped, reaching down to grip Hux's hair, dig her nails into Richard's shoulder through his jacket. "Please! Please just do it."

As Hux began to lick the outer lips of her pussy, nipping the flesh, massaging with his tongue and then his fingers, Richard swirled his tongue around her clitoris. He made a low moan in his throat before he began to suck, faster and harder, building the sensation as a wave that would overtake her.

"Hux," she grunted, twisting out of control. He glanced up at her, though he never stopping touching her. "Please put your fingers inside of me. I want to feel you."

He nodded and stretched her, first with one finger, then two, finally with three. He pumped slowly, in time to Richard's pulls on her sensitive clitoris. And the wall that had been building began to crumble. She tried to fight it, tried to think of something else to stave off the explosion, but there was only this and them and the powerful pleasure that stole every other thought and reason in her mind.

"I'm going to come," she cried out. "Please let me come. I need to come."

Richard nipped her clitoris. "Then come for me. I want to feel it and taste it and hear it shake these walls. I want every servant in my employ to know that you shattered beneath us."

He returned his tongue to her and stroked harder, faster. She arched out of control as the pleasure ripped her almost in two. Waves of it hit her, her body contracting around Hux's fingers as he stroked her through the release. She let out a sound that was animal and didn't care that it echoed in the room. The pleasure, denied by these men even as they tormented her with its promise, was too big to be contained. She rode it out for what felt like a lifetime, shaking and jolting and swearing as sweat poured down her forehead and her hips thrust against Richard's tongue.

Hux slowed his thrusts and sucks, as did Richard, easing her down from the mountaintop together as her convulsions turned to mere shudders. When she lay still and spent, Richard caught her hands and pulled her to a seated position. He moved out of the way as he wrapped her arms around Hux's neck. Hux cupped her backside, shifting so that he could bring her into his lap, her legs around his hips, cradling her against him as he kissed her lips and cheeks and neck.

"You are a goddess," he murmured against her ear. "I could watch you come forever."

She smiled against the rough fabric of his coat but was too weak to respond. Still, she felt the hardness of his cock between her legs. After a few moments in his arms, she flexed against it, rotating her hips to tease him as he had teased her. He grunted and laughed as he drew back to look at her. "Always ready?"

"For you? Do you have to ask, Huxley?"

Richard made a soft sound behind them and she glanced over her shoulder. He had shifted to the bed behind her, lying propped up on the pillows. He was watching them, almost as if he couldn't look away. And like Hux, his cock was outlined against his trousers.

"Take it out," she said. "Touch it."

His eyes widened. "That's what you want?"

"I want to see it. And I know he wants to, as well. I want to feel it."

Hux tilted her head back and claimed her lips, kissing her hard, harder than he normally did. She returned the kiss, their tongues warring for a moment and then he broke away and looked at Richard. "I'd certainly be interested in the same, Richard."

"Then I couldn't deny you," Richard said with a half-smile as he unfastened his trousers and drew out the hard cock beneath.

Zara swallowed hard as she looked over her shoulder at him, her mouth watering. He was something to behold, after all. Thick and hard, the head of him swollen and leaking just a hint of come. She licked her lips and he shook his head with a chuckle.

"You're a menace," he whispered. "And you know it."

"Then I suppose," she said, lifting against Hux again, grinding against him through his trousers, "that you two better figure out how to punish me for that. Wouldn't you say?"

CHAPTER 6

Hux

H ux knew how much Zara liked sex. Liked pleasure. It was
something she had rebuilt, that he had helped her find
again, after the nightmare of how they had started. And that was
why he loved watching her come so much. Why he never asked
for anything but for her pleasure. Because it was a glorious battle
in a war that he knew some never won. She staked her claim in
pleasure, met demons head on and declared, "You will have no
more."

He had never respected anyone more for something.

Not to mention that the results of her exploration of desire
were always of great benefit to him. Even now as she rocked
against him, grinding down on his cock, he was on fire.

She turned away from Richard and looked at him, their eyes
locking. She smiled just a little, something that was only his.
"Undress," she said softly, then added more loudly, "Both of you
undress."

Hux didn't have to be asked twice. He shifted her off his lap
and stood while Richard did the same. Zara moved to her knees

on the bed and leaned forward on her hands, watching with intensity as the two men stepped closer to each other.

Hux drew in a shaky breath and looked at Richard too. He still had his hard cock in his hand and he stroked it once as he met Hux's gaze. Hux shivered and found himself reaching out, tangling his fingers with Richard's so they pulled his cock together once, twice.

"Too much of that and Zara won't get what she so richly deserves," Richard said, his voice low and thick. He cupped the back of Hux's neck and drew him down so their mouths met. They kissed for a moment, tongues tangling and stroking along each other, and then Richard stepped back. "But I do want much, much more of that later."

Hux nodded, too dizzy to speak. "Then at least let me assist you with your clothing," he murmured at last.

He caught the edges of Richard's jacket and pulled him a little closer. Richard gasped but didn't resist as he was pulled flush against Hux. Hux reached around, letting his hands slide down the other man's back, over his hips, his muscular backside. He moved Richard even closer, reveling in the hardness of his bare cock against his trousers.

As he did so, Richard wedged his hands between them and began to unfasten Hux's jacket. He pushed it away, then went to work on the linen shirt beneath. Hux smiled at Richard's intense focus, at the shortness of his breath. Two could play this game.

He went to work on Richard's clothing. They were silent, just unfastening, pushing, lifting shirts away. And all the while Zara watched, her hand between her legs, playing lightly as she stared at them undressing each other. Hux knew he should put on a show for her. Under any other circumstances, he would. But right now he was too swept up in the way Richard's fingers stroked over his ribcage when he pushed Hux's shirt up. Or the feel of the soft curls on Richard's chest when Hux slid his hands down to the waist of the other man's already unfastened trousers.

Richard drew him in for another kiss, this time slow and easy, deep and drugging. Hux knew his trousers were being unfastened, felt Richard's magical fingers lower the fall front, felt him tug Hux's hard cock free. The warm air in the room mingled with the heat of the other man's hand, and Hux sighed into Richard's mouth at the erotic sensation of him gently tugging the turgid flesh.

They broke the kiss but remained in each other's space, staring at each other as Richard continued to slowly stroke Hux's cock, smoothing his thumb over the tip.

"Do you fuck her arse?" he asked.

Hux blinked and tried to clear his addled mind to understand the question. Her arse.

"Yes," Zara answered for him. "He does."

Richard smiled at her and increased the pace of his hand on Hux's cock. Hux felt the rising swell of pleasure in his balls, the edge of release that was so close he could almost taste it. Taste the other man like he could still taste Zara on his tongue. He let out a low moan without meaning to.

"May I?" Richard asked Zara.

Hux looked back at her and found her enthusiastically nodding. "Together?" she murmured, pleaded.

"Most definitely." Richard shoved Hux's trousers away and stroked him one last, firm time. Then he turned him to face Zara. "Make her shake for you."

Hux didn't have to be told twice. He was so close to the edge now, he needed to fuck something, and Zara was always his first choice. He joined her in the bed, moving to rest his back against the pillows. She crawled back into his lap, straddling his cock just as she had been a moment before. As she lowered herself, taking him into her wet body inch by slow inch, she cupped his cheeks.

"I love watching him touch you," she whispered. "I love hearing you moan, Huxley. Moan for me."

He did so because he had no choice. Her words, the feel of her wrapping around him like second skin, the vision of Richard over her shoulder, shucking his own trousers away and then moving to retrieve a bottle of oil from a bedside table…it was all too much.

She crushed her mouth to his, tangling her tongue with his as she flexed over him in slow, steady thrusts. She gripped him and pleasure arched up his cock, making starbursts explode on the edges of his vision. He had fucked this woman so many times and every time it was a marvel to feel her clench around him, to hear her gasp and sigh with pleasure as she ground against him. It was heaven and he could die happy this way, with her.

He felt the weight of Richard joining them on the bed. Hux widened his legs to give the other man room and shivered when Richard touched his bare calves, let his fingers slide up to his thighs as he positioned himself behind Zara.

She whimpered, breaking the contact of their mouths as she looked back at Richard. Together she and Hux watched as he kissed her shoulder, his teeth nipping gently. He pressed his fingers between the globes of her arse and she gripped Hux's cock harder with a harsh wail. He buried his face against her neck, sucking her flesh, fingers digging into her back as he rocked her harder against him.

He wanted to come so very badly, to fill her up as she convulsed around him, but there was something glorious that was about to happen and he didn't want to miss it. And as if that heated thought conjured Richard, Hux felt the first press of him as he pushed his cock against Zara's backside. Hux held still, pressing kisses against her neck and murmuring meaningless sounds of encouragement as she took the other man inch by impressive inch.

Hux could feel Richard's cock stoking his through the thin wall between Zara's pussy and arse, feel the length and heat of him as Richard balanced against Hux's shoulders and groaned his pleasure at the tight fit of her.

Once he was fully seated, Richard raised his gaze, found Hux's, and together they began to move. It was overwhelming. The flex of Zara around them, the rub of each other, the slick heat of sweat and oil and the remnants of her pleasure from what they'd done before. Fingers tangled, legs brushed, mouths sought, and it didn't matter whose belonged to whom. They were one now, one ball of increasing pleasure.

Hux had been in such situations before. With Zara, even. But this was different. Somehow it was different when it was Richard Fitzroy who drove into her and into the heart of Hux's pleasure and desire. Richard Fitzroy who was so dangerous and so tempting and already so aware of exactly what the two of them truly were. No other lover they'd taken had seen them so fully before.

It was perilous to think that, so Hux pushed it aside and focused instead on sensation, on drawing Zara to the edge, on the slide of Richard inside her. And on the orgasm he felt boiling hotter and faster in his balls.

Zara threw her head back, resting it against Richard's shoulder as her breath shortened. Hux could feel the change in her, the desperation that entered her clenching thrusts as she edged toward release. He watched her, fascinated as always by the flush that crept down her chest and the way her lips parted in a silent scream that always seemed to precede the not-so-silent one. That sound tore from her lips now as her pussy began to clench in wave after wave of deep pleasure.

"Fuck," Hux gasped, gripping her hips, trying to find purchase in the never-ending sensations that these two people were creating in him. Now there was no holding back, no stopping the pleasure as it sizzled up his balls.

He came, gripping Zara harder, gasping out her name. Richard leaned forward over her shoulder and captured the sound with his lips, kissing Hux hard. Hux felt him come, as well, the ripple of his pleasure matching Hux's own as their tongues tangled and their hands sought each other and her between them.

She collapsed over Hux with a sob when it was over, her fingers clenching against his back. She whimpered when Richard pulled from her body and rolled to lie beside them, stroking her skin and Hux's skin like he was trying to memorize the shape of them.

Hux wanted to stay cogent, to stay aware and awake. But it had been a long time since he had surrendered himself so utterly, and he found the soft flex of her fingers and Richard's fingers and the warmth of the fire and the sound of the breath of his two lovers was overpowering. He slid into sleep at last, content, at least for a moment.

And that moment was enough for now.

CHAPTER 7

Zara

Zara woke to faint light coming around the edges of the curtains in a room she didn't recognize. At first she tensed, dragged back to so many mornings when she'd woken in places that she didn't know, that sometimes weren't safe. But then she recalled in rapid succession, the pleasures of the previous night. And she smiled.

Her body ached, but it was a good ache. A well-used, well-pleased ache that came from two men entirely focused on her pleasure. She rolled over to find Hux beside her in the big bed. But Richard was gone.

Hux was asleep, and she examined him in the dimness. She had seen his surrender last night and it was remarkable. Watching him pleasured by another person, another man, was always moving. But it had felt...different...with Richard. Like he was drawing out some part of Hux that he normally hid, even from her.

Hux opened one eye. "I can almost hear you overthinking."

She laughed and leaned up to kiss him before she settled into his open arms. "I can hear you overthinking, too."

"Well, it's a...unique situation," Hux said slowly. His fingers began to thread through her hair, stroking through the locks and against her scalp gently. "We've indulged in heady pleasures like this before, but never with a man who..."

"Who knows what we are? Who is the kind of man with the power to destroy us?" Zara said, glancing at the door.

Hux nodded. "Yes."

She pondered that statement for a moment. It was true, of course. Richard was a gentleman, with obvious power and wealth. The two of them were thieves and liars, making their way by often illegal or at least what would be considered unsavory means. A man like Richard could break them with a flick of his wrist.

"I know you don't trust him and maybe I'm a fool. But Hux, I don't think he *wants* to destroy us," she said softly, and then looked up at Hux.

His expression was troubled as he stared straight across the room at the embers of the fire that glowed in the distance. She sensed the pleasure that remained in him after last night just as it remained in her. But she also sensed his worry. His concern. She sensed a great deal in him in that moment, so much that he normally hid from her in some attempt to protect her.

But things had changed last night. She knew it. She'd felt it when the two men touched her, when she'd watched them touch each other. The world had shifted, and now she wondered if it was possible for them to hide anymore. If this was the moment they could come into the light together in some new way and maybe, just maybe...change?

She cleared her throat and traced a pattern on his bare pectoral muscle. "Hux?"

"Mmmm?"

She wanted to look at him but couldn't quite dare to do it.

"Were you...were you ever embarrassed about my history as the Countess. As a lightskirt?"

He jolted beneath her, and when she forced herself to look up, she found his dark eyes wide. "Where is that coming from, Zara?"

She shrugged. "I...it was just something about the way you reacted at the beginning, when Richard made his initial offer."

Hux's expression softened and he reached down to trace her lips with his fingertip. "Zara Cooper, I have never been nor could I ever be embarrassed by you. I'm...I'm proud of all you are and all you have ever been. I'm proud of all you overcame."

Relief rushed through her at that statement. She'd always thought he felt that way, aside from that brief moment the previous day. But this was the first time they'd ever discussed it. And now it was like a floodgate opened. She wanted to say everything. Even the things that she feared.

"Because of you," she whispered.

He stiffened further and shook his head but didn't respond. His twisted expression almost made it seem like he couldn't respond. Like he feared what would happen if he did.

She sat up and turned to look at him. She needed to look at him now. "Hux," she began slowly. "You must know that I—"

She didn't get to finish. He caught her arms and drew her forward, catching her mouth in a kiss. She didn't fight him, she never had, she never would or could. He swept her away and she wanted to be caught in his tide.

But she knew his tricks. This pleasure was a wall so she wouldn't declare her heart. He didn't want it, even if he wanted her.

And that stung more than it should have. Still, she relaxed into him, letting the kiss grow deeper and with more purpose. She wanted him and if he only wanted her and nothing more, that had been enough for years. She couldn't risk that just so she could say emotions that he considered foolish or unrequited.

She moved over him, straddling his waist, and he moaned

against her throat as he traced the line of her pulse with his tongue. She clenched her legs around him at the sensation of his hot mouth on her skin. There would never be a time that this remarkable man didn't move her. She had to remember that and not get caught up in whatever foolish notions she had about what they should share beyond passion and friendship and protection.

He reached between them, his breath short as he positioned himself at her entrance. She adjusted and he slid in without difficulty. They sighed together and she began to grind into his lap, sinking into pleasure that erased all other thought immediately.

There was no sound but the wet slap of their bodies coming together and the occasional pop and hiss of the dying fire behind them. Zara leaned back and Hux put a hand on each breast, massaging them as she increased her pace over him, balancing herself just on the edge of yet another orgasm. But before her body could find that release, there was a sound of a clearing through behind them.

"My, my, what a sight to see," Richard said as he closed the chamber door behind them. He was wearing a dressing gown but clearly nothing else beneath it if the outline of his cock against the fabric was any indication.

Zara lifted her breasts a little farther and didn't slow the pace of her grinding. She just let him watch, his blue eyes dilating, his hands clenching at his sides like he wanted to reach out for them. And she hoped he would give into the impulse. She wanted to feel his skin on hers as she came around Hux's cock. In a very short time, that had become a need, not just a wish.

Richard smiled at her and then looked past her at Hux. Hux was watching him in return, his breath nonexistent now. She shivered at the power of this connection. This unexpected drive to just drown in these two men and watch them drown in each other. It was thrilling and terrifying all at once.

Because she and Hux didn't surrender themselves, not truly. And she feared what would happen if they took that risk with this man. Would they be lost? Or perhaps more frightening, was it possible they could be found?

Richard

R ichard didn't think he'd ever stop being shocked at how much he liked watching Hux and Zara fuck. There was something effortless to their connection. They knew how to give each other pleasure and they did so easily and without games. Zara's skin flushed as she rode Hux, Hux's fingers flexed against her breasts. They were a symphony, a ballet, a show Richard wanted to observe over and over again.

And participate in, of course. Watching only took him so far. He untied his robe and tossed it aside. Zara threw her head back, eyes shut in pleasure, but Hux continued to watch Richard. Watch as Richard caught his own cock and began to stroke in time to the thrusts of the couple before him.

Zara shattered within a few moments, her body bending and twisting against Hux, her cries and pants like music in the air around them. She continued to shudder over Hux, even as she collapsed against his chest and he reached up to smooth her hair.

Only then did Richard move to them. He stopped at the bedside and tucked a finger under her chin, turning her face up toward him. She smiled, her expression almost dreamy. He leaned in and kissed her, soft at first, but then with more force, with more demand. His fingers tangled into her hair and then he lightly tugged. She jolted against Hux, her faltering sigh proof that she liked his firmer hand.

He let his hands run down her body, pinching her nipples, scraping her back lightly with his nails. All the time, Hux watched, seemingly both concerned and mesmerized by what Richard was doing. Richard's brow wrinkled. The man was always on the edge of fighting to protect Zara, even when she wasn't in danger. He hadn't heard the answer to why yet. Perhaps he never would. That didn't mean he wasn't curious about what made the other man's dark eyes light up with just the edge of anger whenever Richard danced along the edge of what might be a boundary.

"Do you like watching this?" he asked softly, the question directed at Hux. "Like seeing me touch her?"

Hux sucked in a breath and then gave a jerky nod.

Richard smiled. "Do you want me to touch you, Huxley?"

Zara's eyes flew open and she made a strangled sound of desire. Hux opened and shut his mouth a few times before he managed to choke out, "Yes."

"Do you want me to fuck you?" Richard clarified, resting a hand on Hux's thigh, teasing his fingers down the thick, corded length of muscle there.

"Yes," Zara moaned.

Richard laughed. "We have her vote. But I don't take what isn't offered, Hux." He held the other man's stare evenly, daring him to believe it now like he hadn't believed it yesterday. Knowing some part of him wouldn't, even if he said yes. "Do you want me to take you?"

"Yes! I want you."

That confession, gasped on shaky breath, weakened Richard's knees. He hadn't known Hux long, but everything about him said he was a man in control at all times. Perhaps not cautious, but always intensely aware of every move being made. And now he lay back on the pillows, Zara still arching around him, his gaze foggy and unfocused with desire. And he wanted Richard to fuck him.

Richard moved down on the bed, taking a place between Hux's thighs. Zara slowed her strokes, watching over her shoulders and adjusting as Richard tilted Hux up, revealing the balls tight with pleasure against his flesh and the arse that was so entirely tempting.

"Delightful," Richard said, tracing in the puckered hole with the edge of his nail and eliciting a shuddering, gulping cry from Hux. Oh yes, he was going to enjoy this. "Zara, love, get that oil from the bedside table there, will you?"

Zara nodded and reached over without breaking contact, grabbing the bottle of oil the men had used on her last night. She handed it back and continued to rock over Hux, teasing him even as Richard started doing the same.

He poured oil on his fingers, warming it between them, and then gently probed Hux's arse. Circling the sensitive hole, then spreading it with a finger, two. Hux began to lift against Zara and she ground down harder, pressing her hands into his shoulders with sobbing moans and cries of her own.

He pulsed onward, opening Hux, readying him until Hux let out his breath in a desperate huff. "Just do it already!"

Richard laughed and withdrew his fingers, stroking his cock over the hole instead. Hux lifted against him, urging him to press forward. And God, he couldn't wait anymore. His delightful torment of the other man had turned into self-torture. One he needed to end just to cool the burning in his blood that screamed at him to take, claim, own these two people who were too wild to be tamed. To keep them even though that wasn't arrangement, could never be the arrangement.

He ignored the tangled emotions and instead focused on the heavenly feeling as he pressed forward and slowly breached Hux's tight, hot body, claiming him at last and in the process losing just the tiniest part of himself. But it didn't matter—all that mattered was this.

So he began to thrust.

~

Hux

Hux's vision blurred with pleasure so intense he couldn't think straight. His cock was being milked by a woman who meant more to him than anyone else in the world and a sensual man, almost a stranger, was fucking him in the arse with long, certain strokes that hit exactly the right places every time.

It was all too much. He twisted on the sheets, grunting and wailing, lost to everything but the never-ending pulse of pleasure they were creating in his body. They played him like a fiddle, matching their strokes, writhing with their own musical sounds of desire, and it was everything that mattered in the world. All that there was.

He looked up at Zara, watching her as she swung her head back and forth with the ride. Her nipples were puckered, her body shining with sweat and the glow of passion. Richard leaned forward, driving farther into Hux as he nipped his teeth over her shoulder and then gently wrapped a hand around her throat.

Her eyes flew open, and for a moment Hux froze, staring at the image. Was it fine for her? Was she frightened? Did he need to intervene?

But she smiled, lifting her hands to Richard's and tightening his fingers with her own, just a fraction. Richard drove harder into Hux and Zara gripped him tighter and they went on, closer to the edge than ever before.

He knew Zara was close, he could see it on her face. Once she had come once, she was always even more sensitive and the overstimulation of the environment, plus her grinding strokes made her pussy begin to pulse wildly, gripping him in pure, wet bliss as he watched her writhe in pleasure.

He wanted to come, he needed it, but just as he got close, Richard dropped his hand away from Zara's throat and down her back. Hux felt him wrap two fingers around the base of his cock in a tight circle.

"Oh no," Richard purred. "Not yet."

Hux bucked against him, against her still pulsing body. He didn't normally take orders from men. And yet Richard's denial excited him on some core level that he didn't fully understand. His control was being stripped away, leaving him at Richard's mercy.

Dangerous. But Hux wasn't afraid of danger.

"Climb off of him, Zara," Richard said softly, "and put him in your mouth. I want him to be able to see me as I do this. I want *you* to be in control of when he spends."

Zara glanced down at Hux, her expression heavy with desire. But also a question. A request for permission, consent. Hux gave it with a nod and she smiled as she slung her leg over him and slithered to the ground beside the bed. She caught him in her hand, holding tight enough to curb his orgasm but not hard enough to hurt. She lowered her mouth over him, swirling her tongue in a teasing thrust.

Now that she wasn't seated on him, Hux had a clear view of Richard, up on his knees, Hux's backside pressed into his thighs, his legs bunched around Richard's armpits. Richard held his stare as he stroked, deeper, slower, toying with Hux. Making him quake in Zara's mouth.

She looked up at him, watching him. But every time he edged close to release, she gripped him just so and the edge faded away, making him chase it again. This went on for what felt like an eternity, and he shivered at being at the complete mercy of his two lovers.

"I want to make him come," Zara said, lifting her head from his lap and looking at Richard.

Richard's face was red with exertion and holding back his own pleasure and he nodded. "I don't think I can torment any of us any longer."

With that Zara and Richard both began to work him in earnest. Richard's thrusts increased and he circled his hips to stimulate Hux further. Zara took him deeper in her throat, moaning around him and dragging him right to the precipice all over again. Only this time, when the pleasure peaked and his legs began to shake, no one stopped him.

He came in a roar of pleasure, pumping hot into Zara's throat as she took every drop. His release seemed to free Richard, because he also made a low groan and withdrew from Hux's arse, coming on his stomach as he let out a series of garbled curses.

Richard collapsed over him, his head near Hux's ribcage. Zara laid herself over his body and he wrapped his arms around her as she tangled her legs in his.

How long they all lay there, struck mute by pleasure, he couldn't have said. It felt like a moment, it felt like a lifetime. He never wanted it to end was all he knew. There were few times that he felt the comfort of surrender. When he did...it was hard to go back to a life led with constant vigilance.

But at last Richard lifted his head, peppering Hux's side and then Zara's shoulder with light, shiver-inducing kisses. "I'm surprised neither of you asked where I was this morning."

Zara laughed, the vibration of it rumbling through Hux. "We were all a little busy for small talk. So where were you?"

"Well, we slept the morning away," Richard said. "So I was arranging for our luncheon. Which..." He glanced over at the clock on the mantel. "We are already late for, I fear."

Hux laughed at the idea that they were on a timetable. And once he started, he couldn't stop. Zara joined in and then Richard, though the other's man's full laugh seemed a little rusty. But they laughed together and it was wonderful.

"Shall we clean up and dress, then?" Zara asked at last. "With our apologies to the staff?"

"I suppose I could eat," Hux said, his stomach grumbling as if on cue. "Food first, then one or both of you."

Zara leaned up and kissed him. "Sounds perfect."

And Hux realized, in that warm and close moment...that it very nearly was.

CHAPTER 8

Hux

The lunch was worth the wait, for the spread was amazing—
too much food for three people, even ones made ravenous
by sex and sin. But even as Hux devoured all on his plate, he
keenly felt the disparity in his position to Richard. He was a man
who had grown up unable to waste even a scrap of food. Starva-
tion had always been a possibility long into his adulthood.

But Richard, he could dispose of piles of uneaten food in the
alleyways and never think once about what he'd lost versus what
he had.

Hux leaned back in his chair and watched Zara and Richard
talking. She was leaning forward, entirely engaged in the
subject...he thought it was some book they had both read. Hux
hadn't. He had only come to reading late in life, taught by Zara, in
fact. While he enjoyed the endeavor, he much preferred when she
read something to him, her face animated by the story.

But now she had found an equal in that pursuit and she was
animated as they dissected the piece. They looked...easy together.

Just as they did when Richard was touching her...kissing her. A twinge of something like jealousy tingled through Hux's body.

He hated himself for it. After all, he'd never thought he could have Zara forever. She'd turned to him during a terrible point in her life, but one day she might find someone who could offer her more than stealing from balls or dancing in the rain behind gaming halls. A man like the one who was pouring her more wine, laughing at something clever she had said. Someone cultured and safe and able to offer a future that was steady.

Hux had always planned on letting her go eventually, which was part of why he never allowed himself to get too close. Why he cut off his feelings and any misguided attempt she made to express her own. Saying them would only make it harder in the long run.

As for the other part of why he kept her at arm's length? It was simple, after all. He didn't trust emotions like love. He didn't trust much of anything at all. He'd seen too much in his life that proved people would only disappoint. He didn't want to be disappointed. And more so, he didn't want to disappoint her.

He looked at Richard. As for him...well, Hux might ache deliciously from the man's attention, but that didn't mean he knew him. Didn't mean he wouldn't keep a solid eye on him. And that he wouldn't forget him when this was over. He had to forget him.

He shifted and shook his head. Being lost in thought was no good for anyone. He pushed his shoulders back and said, "So, Fitzroy, I have a question."

Richard turned away from Zara and faced Hux, his brows lifted. "Back to Fitzroy, are we?"

Hux shifted. Calling the man by his first name when they were tangled in each other's arms was one thing. Somehow it felt too intimate when they weren't fucking. "You do not wish to know the question?"

Now Zara set her fork down and stared at Hux with wide eyes.

But if Richard took offense to the attitude, he didn't show it. "Ask away. I think we've all earned a little transparency."

Hux fought not to flinch at the very vulnerability he'd been pondering. The same vulnerability he was incapable of sharing. The way Richard stared, it was as if he could read Hux's mind. That was a troubling thought after such a short, if passionate, acquaintance.

"You said that you assumed at some point Zara and I would try to steal something from you. Did you make sure I would discover and attempt to pilfer your late wife's brooch?"

Richard held his stare for a long moment, then looked at Zara. "You two think me quite the Machiavelli."

Zara's brow lowered. "Did you?" she pressed.

Richard took a sip of his wine before he answered. "After I realized what you two were doing at the party last week, after I realized what I wanted and invited you here, I certainly don't deny that I wanted what has happened to happen. That I wanted to make an offer to you both to share in some pleasure."

"That's avoiding the question. Us stealing the emerald and you asking us for this affair are separate things. You said so yourself, that you weren't coercing either one of us through threats."

"True." Richard sipped his wine. He held himself stiffly and Hux narrowed his gaze. Richard was uncomfortable. It didn't bode well.

"You acted strangely when we arrived," Zara said, glancing at Hux briefly. "Both of us noted it. And you left us quite suddenly, but caught us immediately upon our taking the item. Almost as if you had laid a trap."

"Is this his interrogation or yours, my dear?" Richard asked.

"We're a matched set," Hux said softly. "It is a valid observation. I am only curious."

"I didn't hide the emerald," Richard said after a hesitation that felt like it lasted a lifetime. "I knew it would be a temptation if you went snooping."

"You wanted us to attempt to steal it," Zara said slowly. "Why? How does that play into it."

To his surprise, some of the life bled from Richard's expression. He shifted slightly and tapped his fingers along the table for a moment before he said, "I suppose the simplest answer is that I wanted to feel alive again. Because I...I lost my wife several years ago. She and my son died in childbirth. And I was lost. I almost ended it all."

Zara jolted a little, but Hux managed to keep his visceral reaction to that statement from his face. He still felt the ricochet of pain, though.

"Oh," Zara whispered.

Richard's jaw tightened. "Yes. It was a dark time."

He stared off past them, out the dining room window, though Hux didn't think for a moment that he was seeing anything except his memories. His grief. His fingers flexed against the table because he wanted so badly to reach across the space between them and touch this man. Comfort him. Instead, he fisted his hand against the tabletop.

"How did you recover?" Zara asked, her tone so gentle.

"I've learned time is the only friend to those in mourning," Richard said with a sad smile. "The pain returns, of course. It is a constant that will probably be in my life for the rest of my days. But it isn't as sharp now. Ultimately, I felt ready to enter the world again."

"And we were your entrée?" Hux asked, eyes going wide.

Richard laughed. "Lord, no. That would have been diving a bit too deeply to start, don't you think? I've had lovers here and there in the past year. But I admit it all felt rote. Disconnected. As if I were simply scratching an itch or filling my belly for the sake of function alone. Until I saw you two at the party."

"Stealing?" Hux asked, incredulous.

"Yes. And fucking," Richard said coolly.

Hux was glad he'd set his fork down, for he surely would have dropped it at that statement. "Fucking?" he repeated, and looked at Zara. She seemed just as shocked as he was, her eyes wide.

"In the parlor," Richard continued.

"Bullshit," Hux said, and shook his head. "I would have seen you."

"Yes, you'd think you would, Hux." Richard leaned closer. "You with your constant vigilance. But one of the most interesting things about you is that if you are near Zara, you occasionally forget everything else."

Hux tensed. It felt like Richard had cut his chest open and revealed his heart. "Where were you?" he asked.

"In the corner of the room, a part hardly touched by firelight." Richard reached out and traced his fingertips along Zara's arm, and she shivered. "I might have gotten up, announced myself and slipped out. But everything happened so fast. I realized you two were thieves and watched you place the spoils of your night on Zara's body and then took her…it was infinitely arousing."

Zara was trembling now and Hux was certain not all of it was about excitement. "Knowing we stole things from your friends made you…aroused?"

"They aren't my friends," Richard corrected. "At least not most of them. And yes, the confidence you both showed, the bravado, the absolute reckless abandon in both your actions and the way you came together afterward was very arousing. There was something magical about it, the way you two connected. And for the first time in years I wanted something more than a mere body to bury myself in for a night with no thought of it again. I wanted *you*." He held his gaze on Hux for a beat, then let it shift to Zara. "And *you*."

Zara shivered and Hux couldn't help but do the same. It was like this man could pin him with a look, hold him steady without effort. No one but Zara had ever been able to do that, and it had taken them months to get to that point. A short time alone with

Richard and he felt like part of himself was left to this man. Controlled by him.

Hux clenched his jaw. He didn't want to be controlled. That was too dangerous. His next words were sharp. "So you want to, what...be a tourist to our criminal activity? Play a little game with what we have been forced to do thanks to the actions of men like you?"

Richard didn't flinch. His expression remained gentle in the face of Hux's harshness. "I know what you do is dangerous. But come now, Huxley, you must admit that you, yourself, are aroused by the game. It's obvious by the way you move when you're on the hunt, by the way you lose control when you see what you've taken resting against her perfect skin."

Hux cleared his throat, which was suddenly thick. "I can't deny it."

"I wanted some taste of that," Richard said with a shrug. "I was willing to be reckless to obtain what I desired. More time with you. A taste of the thrill of what you two do. Who you are."

"That action takes quite a bit of trust," Zara said. She was watching Hux rather than Richard, though. Reading him, he thought, as she could so easily do. "We could hurt you."

"That is always true when you enter into any relationship," Richard said with a shake of his head. "And in truth, I have nothing to lose. Whatever material things you could still steal don't matter. There is nothing more that anyone could take from me that hasn't already been taken. So I'm willing to bargain for what I want without certainty." He locked gazes with her. "Am I wrong?"

Zara caught her breath and glanced at Hux. Richard followed her stare and arched a brow in Hux's direction. "Am. I. Wrong?" he repeated succinctly.

There were a thousand things that Hux could have said in that moment that he knew would cut this arrangement off. Another thousand he could have said to continue it but put an end to this uncomfortable vulnerability. And yet he couldn't say any of them. No matter how dangerous he knew the situation to be, he couldn't let it go. Couldn't let Richard go, or the way it felt to have Richard and Zara together in his life.

So he cleared his throat and ground out, "There is no reason for us to betray you. I know you and Zara agreed to a week together. I do the same."

Richard didn't respond, but held his gaze instead. The silence drew out between them, as did the way Hux was drawn in by the blue of the other man's stare. One could get lost in this man. Never be found.

Finally, he looked away, and only then did Richard say, "Then we understand each other."

They continued their luncheon and Richard changed the subject, returning to lighter topics like music, but Hux felt a lingering sense of unease. The conversation between them had not gone badly, and yet he felt like he'd...lost something.

At last the plates were cleared and Richard sat back in his chair with a smile for both Zara and Hux. "I have a suggestion for an afternoon entertainment."

Hux snorted out a laugh. "I'm sure you do."

Zara leaned forward and let her fingers trace Richard's hand. Richard's pupils dilated with the action and she whispered, "And what is that?"

"How about a spirited game of Vingt-un?"

At the suggestion, Hux nearly spit out the sip of wine he'd just taken. "The card game?" he asked.

Richard shrugged. "There will be plenty of time for other entertainments later. Sometimes the truest pleasure is just...waiting. Anticipating."

"I've always loved a game of cards," Zara said with a shake of her head as she set her napkin on the table. "I'm game."

"I warn you, she's a terrible cheat," Hux said as he got up and came around the table to offer his arm to Zara.

She stood and took it, but swatted him playfully as she did so. "Don't tell him that, you'll ruin the game."

Richard laughed, this time with his full chest, and the sound rang in the room like something beautiful. He motioned his hand toward the door and they all left together, heading to a parlor where they would play their game.

Hux just hoped the larger game was one he wouldn't lose.

CHAPTER 9

Richard

Richard couldn't recall the last time he'd just had...*fun*. And yet, as he, Zara and Hux finished off their last round of cards, that was exactly what he felt. After the passion of the morning and the vulnerability at luncheon, their afternoon of games had been surprisingly easy. They'd talked and laughed, and Richard had gotten glimpses of a deeper side to each of his lovers.

Zara loved reading and her face lit up when they discussed books. Hux was harder to crack, but Richard had come to discover that he liked art. Not just for stealing, but to look at. When Richard had confessed his investment in several of the plays of Peter Reid, a handsome and talented playwright, they had all come to realize they had been at several of the same performances of the man's work.

"Though certainly we were not in anyone's box," Zara said with a laugh.

And Hux had smiled along with her and winked audaciously at Richard. "Unless we snuck in."

The time had flown and now the clock in the hallway gonged

out three. Richard blinked at the realization that the whole day had gone by.

"Tea will be in an hour," he said, setting down his final hand of cards and smiling when he saw Zara had won the round again. Likely because when Hux cheated, it was on her behalf.

Because of course it was.

"I suppose we should all go up and prepare then," Hux said softly, and his gaze glittered as he glanced over at Zara. She gave a knowing smile in return.

Richard tilted his head. "That actually leaves me with a question. You are always impeccable, Zara, but you came with no servants. How do you do it?"

Her smile widened. "We aren't like you, Richard. Having a servant could be dangerous for people like us. You have to trust someone entirely when they can see what you're doing behind the scenes."

"And split what you earn to keep them quiet," Hux added.

"I fix my own hair, but Mr. Huxley has become just as good at dressing me as he has at undressing me," Zara concluded before she leaned over the table, cupped Hux's cheeks and drew him in for a deep kiss.

Richard shifted at the sight of them entangled. It would never grow old, he could see that. It would always excite him to watch them together.

"I would wager he distracts you as often as he assists," he said with a light laugh as they parted.

Hux arched a brow. "Wouldn't you?"

"Absolutely," Richard agreed.

"And that's why we budget for a great deal more time to ready ourselves than perhaps we actually need. So that everyone gets... relief," she said, and then shivered, her pupils dilating.

Richard swallowed. "You know, we could just as easily have tea in my chamber as in some stuffy parlor where we can't be as...comfortable."

"I don't know," Hux said, his hand settling on Richard's knee beneath the table, stroking gently. "It seems to be that we could be very comfortable with her splayed out on a settee, moaning our names while we take turns fucking her."

Richard heard the breath exit his lungs and he playfully glared at Hux for eliciting that response, which in turn made Hux laugh, a husky sound of desire and amusement mixed.

"A very pretty thought," Richard agreed. "But I think I might rather remain in bed the rest of the day where there will be no interruptions."

Zara's face lit up with the idea even as she said, "But the settee another time?"

"Most definitely," Richard said, and got to his feet. There was no hiding the erection that now pressed against the fall front of his trousers. Zara licked her lips at the sight and brushed her hand against it through the heavy fabric, caressing the length of him as she stared up into his eyes.

"Now," Richard said more sharply.

Both Zara and Hux got up at his order, and together they all stumbled back up to the Richard's chamber. Zara turned into Hux, her arms winding around his neck as she lifted on her tiptoes to kiss him. Hux cupped her backside, grinding her against him rhythmically as she gasped and groaned against his lips. But at last she stopped and turned back toward Richard.

"Would you like to see him serve as my attendant? How he readies me?"

"I do like to see him ready you."

She glanced over her shoulder and nodded. Hux's pupils dilated as he reached to unfasten the first button on her gown. "I live to serve, Countess."

Zara let out her breath in a soft sigh and Richard smiled. He knew she had been called the Countess during her days as a light-skirt and courtesan. He had also sensed that there was pain associated with those days, and yet it was evident this wasn't the first time she and Hux had played this game of mistress and servant, of forbidden pleasure.

He was more than willing to be part of it.

"You know," he said as he moved to the bed. "Were you really a countess, the earl might stand by as you were readied by a servant, waiting to take you to his bed."

Zara's gaze had been a bit bleary as Hux slowly undressed her, but now her eyes lifted. "Would he now? Would he be excited as he watched another man take her out of her clothes?"

Richard nodded. "He would be. Watching another man's hands on you? Very arousing. And knowing that same man would then watch the earl fuck his countess...would also be very exciting."

Zara shivered. "It seems only fair, Huxley. After all, poor Richard has watched you take me more than once. Do you want to watch him do the same?"

Huxley leaned forward, pressing gentle kisses along her throat even as he stared at Richard, their gazes locked. "Oh yes," he finally breathed. "But may your loyal servant please himself while you do so?"

"But not come," Richard said, his tone a little sharp, a bit closer to "lord of the manor" command. And Hux's hands hesitated before he slid Zara's dress forward.

"I will do as the gentleman orders," Hux said, and one side of his mouth quirked in a smile.

Richard's cock actually throbbed in response. Oh yes, he liked this game. He thought he might like it just as much when he played the servant and Hux was in control. If he could be coaxed to be in control. He was always so careful not to be, at least with Zara. But Richard wanted to see him desperate and rough—he had a feeling that would be very much something to behold and experience firsthand.

"Then finish undressing her," Richard commanded. "And Zara, get on the bed. Then Huxley, I think I will also need help with my clothing as my valet seems to be missing."

Hux's gaze flitted over Richard in a slow perusal. Then he nodded. "Yes, my lord."

Huxley took his time sliding Zara's dress from her shoulders. As with the previous day, she wasn't wearing underthings, and Richard let himself look at her, drink in her naked curves that felt so fucking good against him.

Slowly Hux moved to his knees, his mouth just barely brushing over her skin as he did so. She let out a little sound of pleasure and gripped his shoulders for purchase as he carefully untied the garter that held up one silk stocking. He rolled it away, his fingers gorgeous against the paler skin of her thighs.

"May I adjust you, my lady?" he asked, looking up at her. "To more easily remove the other stocking?"

"Yes," she breathed, watching him, trembling in anticipation for what he would do next.

He smiled at her, wicked, and then slowly eased on long leg over his shoulder, spreading her open above him, forcing her to lean on him as he pressed his hands to her still-stockinged calf and eased his fingers up the length of her inner thigh.

"Let me just, help you here, my lady," he said softly, and lifted his mouth between her legs.

"Hux," she breathed, fingers coming into his hair as he began to lick her gently, slowly, meant to tease not make her come. But that didn't make it any less arousing to watch him play with her.

"Look at me," Richard said.

She jerked her head up, almost startled. "Yes, my lord," she said. "I'm almost ready."

He nodded, forcing himself back to the game. "Yes, you look to be almost ready. Your servant does a very good job."

"He does," She tilted her head back with a moan. "Oh God, yes, he does. We should share him regularly if your valet is not reliable."

"A very good idea." Richard smiled.

Hux was unfastening Zara's other garter while he licked her, and he tugged her stocking away at last and then drew back, his lips shining with her juices. "Will that be all, my lady?"

Zara swallowed and let her fingers move through his hair as she slowly walked away. "Yes, Huxley. I think you will see to the earl now."

"I will indeed," Hux said, and got to his feet in one graceful, fluid motion. Richard stopped breathing as he moved toward him, all erotic confidence and certainty. This man was...a marvel. And Richard trembled knowing he would touch him. Watch him.

"If you help with the waistcoat, I can manage my cravat and shirt," Richard choked out. "I will need more attention to the trousers."

"Of course, my lord," Hux said, his voice rough.

He caught the edge of Richard's jacket and drew him closer. Close enough that their chests brushed and their mouths almost aligned. Hux wedged his hand between them and just as he had done with Zara earlier, he slowly unfastened each and every button along the brocaded silk vest.

On the bed now, Zara opened her legs and set a hand between them, gently beginning to touch herself as she watched them together. Richard nodded at her. "Yes, ready yourself, my dear. I'll be there shortly."

Her fingers moved more swiftly against her pussy, and she let out a little moan instead of an answer. Richard slid a finger beneath Hux's chin and slowly turned his face to look at her.

"I'm going to have her, Huxley," he said softly, watching how Hux's face changed when he looked at her. "I'm going to make her screech and twist and make my cock wet with her come. While you watch me. Are you ready?"

"Yes," Hux whispered. "Her coming is one of my greatest pleasures."

Richard smiled. "Now the trousers, please."

Huxley inclined his head in acquiescence and stepped back so Richard could shed his jacket, the now-opened waistcoat and the shirt beneath. Hux let his fingers drag down Richard's bare chest and stomach before he caught the edge of his waistband. He let his fingers play there, dipping beneath the fabric, teasing and playing for what felt like an eternity, though in truth it was only a moment.

He unfastened the buttons on Richard's fall front and made a rumbling sound deep in his chest as Richard's hard cock bounced free. Hux caught it, stroking him once, twice. Pleasure ripped through him at the touch, and he thrust into Hux's warm palm almost against his will.

"Fuck," he muttered, and Hux smiled.

"You're going to," Hux said, and in that moment the played façade of servant was gone. With Richard's cock in Hux's hand, he saw a glimpse of someone who could dominate. Take what he wanted, demand pleasure. And it was intoxicating while it lasted. "Fuck her, fuck me, be fucked. That's the entire idea." He stroked again and the moment passed. He shucked Richard's trousers away and stepped back. "Is there anything else I can do for you, my lord?"

Richard wanted this man's mouth on him so badly he could almost feel the flex of Hux's throat. But he pushed that desire away and looked instead at Zara, already arching against her hand on the bed, watching them with her mouth slightly open and her pupils dilated with deep pleasure.

"Just stand by," he said, walking past him, letting his hand trail against Hux's chest as he did. "In case you are needed."

"Anything you wish, my lord, my lady," Hux said, and moved to a chair that faced the bed. He took his place, unfastening his own fall front and pulling his cock—God, that gorgeous cock—free.

Richard swallowed hard at the sight of him but tore himself away to go to Zara. He slid his hands up her calves, her thighs, pressing his fingers against her flesh, denting it as she hissed out pleasure.

"I don't want to make love to you, Zara," he said softly.

Her brow wrinkled. "No?"

"No, I want to fuck you. Take you. Claim you. I want to be rough, animal. I want to mark your skin with him fingers, I want to tug your hair while you buck against me. But only if that is something you'd like."

Behind him, he heard Hux take in a sharp breath, but didn't look at him. Neither did Zara. She stared up at Richard, reading him, judging him. And then...she nodded. "Yes," she whispered. "Use me. I...I *trust* you not to cross a line. To stop if I tell you to do so."

Trust. Richard knew that was not something that either of these two people came by easily. He glanced over to find Hux and saw that his expression said as much. Worry lined the hard angles proving he did not yet fully believe Richard had earned such a thing.

And yet Zara offered it, so he must never, *ever* betray it.

"Immediately," he promised.

She seemed to ponder that and then she nodded. "Then do it. Take me, my lord," she said, falling back into the game. "Show me you own my pleasure. Make him watch you claim me."

He gripped her thighs, pressing his fingers harder into her soft flesh, and then he tugged, sliding her to the edge of the bed and pushing her legs wider so he could see the dripping evidence of her arousal.

"You are mine, my lady," he whispered. "Mine."

She made a garbled sound and gripped the coverlet as he ducked his head and licked her. She was sweet and salty, dripping with desire, and he sucked her clitoris first gently, then harder, forcing her to arch against him as she wailed out pleasure. He pulled back before she could come and scraped his teeth against the hard nub.

"Mine," he repeated, and caught her hands, moving her to a seated position perched on the edge of the high bed. He wrapped a hand around the back of her neck, pulled her forward and claimed her mouth, rough and forceful. She didn't resist. She hands raked along his chest, nails leaving marks there that made him shiver. It seemed she wanted to be as rough as he had offered to be.

He dug his fingers into her hair, tilting her face, holding her steady as he kissed her again, deep and fast, thrusting with his tongue until she rocked against him with a shuddering moan.

"Please," she murmured.

"Oh yes," he said with a smile. "Beg me, Countess. Beg me for what you want."

"Just take me," she whimpered.

"Oh no, not so easy as that," he said, releasing her. "First I want to feel what you can do with that remarkable mouth. With that delectable throat."

Her eyes widened and then a wicked smile crossed her lips. "So you challenge me to steal *your* control."

"If you can," he said, though he knew she would. But he wanted her on her knees, wanted Hux to watch him fuck her mouth while she teased herself with her fingers.

She slithered to the ground and then nipped his lower lip. Not hard enough to draw blood, but he felt the sharpness. "With pleasure."

She started to drag her mouth down his body, scraping a nipple with her teeth, feeling him with her hands, down, down, always sucking and licking lower and lower as she looked up at him, watching him react. At last she came to her knees and she stroked his cock with her hand like Hux had.

Richard looked at Hux, who was perched far forward on the seat, his own cock in his hand. He wasn't moving, though, he was just staring. Richard angled her head a little so Hux could have a better view when she took him in her mouth.

And then he forgot about everything in the room but her.

CHAPTER 10

Zara

Z ara had always liked a cock in her mouth. Well, a cock of a man she trusted, anyway. One she wanted. And she wanted Richard, quite desperately. She liked how he was forceful with her, like she was something to claim. To take. To devour. Her legs shook when he maneuvered her, she wanted more of it.

And she did, somehow, trust that he could be given carte blanche to be rough without ever hurting her. To claim without stealing. Because the line could be so very thin.

She glanced over and saw Hux watching them. Watching her as she swirled her tongue around another man's cock. He looked aroused and almost feral...he also looked worried. Concerned for her well-being, as always. Her forever protector.

She needed that, too. Needed him. Needed this. It was terrifying and thrilling all at once.

She stroked Richard's cock with her hand while she took him deeper and deeper into her throat. When she had begun a harder, faster rhythm, adjusting to taking more of him, he rested a hand on the back of her head.

"I want to fuck your throat, Zara," he said.

She glanced up at him and nodded around him, relaxing her muscles, gripping his thighs as he thrust into her. Deeper, faster, until her breath was almost stolen by the thickness of him, until tears streamed down her face. Until her body flexed in time to his thrusts and the tingling of pleasure increased until she was ready to explode.

He pulled away and she gasped for breath. Hux sat up straighter.

"Zara—" he began.

"I want this," she interrupted, watching Richard so he understood her consent remained. "I want this."

He caught her hair in his fist, twisting it around and around his hand until she felt the faint sting of the tug. "Take it," he ordered, and his cock was back in her mouth. She watched him as he thrust, his breath short, his grip tightening, a vein in his neck throbbing as he fought for control. She wanted to take that control. To feel him erupt because she had stolen his pleasure.

But suddenly his eyes narrowed and he slowed his hips. "Little minx. Are you trying to control me from your knees?"

She drew back and his cock left her mouth. "I could control you from wherever I please." Hux made a soft sound and she smiled at him. "I could control you both."

"You already do," Hux whispered.

Richard turned her face back and his blue eyes were bright with intensity and challenge. Not angry, not dark, but filled with the excitement of this. The pleasure of this give and take, push and pull. "You will bend, my dear. Right now."

He caught her elbows and brought her up from her knees. He tugged her close and she lifted her mouth, wanting his kiss as much as she longed for his cock. But he denied her that and spun her around, bending her over the bed and pulling her back so that her arse was raised in offering.

She felt his mouth on her sex even before she realized he'd

dropped down behind her. He swirled and licked and stroked, groaning against her, letting her feel the vibrations of his desire through her entire trembling body. He was like fire in her veins, molten lava between her legs, and she ground against his seeking tongue, reaching for pleasure, aching for release that he denied until *he* was ready to gift it.

He rose up at last, caging her in with his arms, sliding one hand under her body so he could stroke her nipples as he aligned himself at her entrance and took her in one long, hard stroke.

"God!" she cried out, pushing back against him, gripping him tighter and reveling in the sensation of being taken.

And he did take. There was nothing soft about what he did, nothing kind. He took her like she was his, like he needed to fuck her as much as he needed to breathe. His hands dug hard, one into her hip, one squeezing her sensitive breast. His mouth buried against her neck and he licked, then nipped. Pleasure and the edge of pain as she fought to match his stride.

"Do you want to come for me?" he asked, moving his hand down her body, between her legs, thrusting harder and faster as he buried his fingers against her clitoris.

"Yes," she moaned, grinding against his hand like an animal in heat.

"Hux," Richard snapped. "Watch her. Come here and watch her come for me."

Zara turned her head, watching Hux move to the bottom of the bed, maneuvering for a better look as Richard thrust harder, faster. He slapped her arse and she shook, the first reverberations of release tipping her ever closer to the edge of madness.

When he flicked her clitoris in steady strokes, she lost all reason. She arched back, holding Hux's gaze as she came in gulping gasps and uncontrolled waves. He leaned over the bed, taking her mouth as she did so, holding her face in his hands, tenderness met with animal desire as she came and came against Richard's seeking cock.

When he came, it was with a harsh roar that seemed to tear the room to shreds. He withdrew from her still-clenching body and spent on her back before he rolled her over and licked her once, twice as she twitched a few last times.

"So sweet," he murmured as together he and Hux placed her onto the bed. She rested her head in Hux's lap as she tried to find some kind of purchase after such a storm, her breath short and her body shaking.

She had come many times in her life, but that was something different. Something powerful. Like she'd found some part of herself to give that she'd never given before.

And she wanted to do it again. Again and again forever.

~

Hux

Hux's cock throbbed as Zara's hair tickled the length of him. He didn't move, though, didn't try to ease the torment. He liked it, for one. Liked the feel of her in his arms and his lap as she recovered from a powerful orgasm.

But also, he was afraid if he moved or breathed or disturbed this moment that both Zara and Richard would see what he felt in it. Pleasure, yes. Desire, yes. But something darker. He felt envious. Not that she fucked another man. No, that was thrilling. He could watch that forever. No, it was that Zara could connect so easily with Richard. That she could trust him after so long of withholding trust for very good reasons.

"Is it his turn?" Zara murmured, turning her face into his bare thigh and kissing it. Her hair dragged along his length and he sucked in a breath.

Richard smiled. "Yes."

He caught her hair again with that firm grip that tugged at the roots. Hux stiffened at the sight of her so manhandled, but she smiled, arched, and he relaxed. She liked this. She wasn't being hurt. She didn't need rescue. He, on the other hand, felt like he was drowning as she rolled over, up onto her knees, and took him into her mouth.

She knew him so well, knew every hitch of his breath, every lift of his hips, every shake of his body. She knew how to bring him pleasure and she did so, sucking and tugging, swirling her tongue around and around until he dropped his head back with a gasping cry. She took him deeper, and Richard pushed her hair back, holding it away so they could both watch her work Hux. Watch him come closer to the edge.

When he fell, he tangled his fingers with Richard's, gripping them both as he pumped into her. She took every drop, licking her lips when it was over before she leaned over to let Richard kiss her. Taste him. And it was almost enough to drive Hux mad with this craving for them all over again.

But it had been a long few days. He was spent with desire and thoughts and drive to possess in a way he'd not felt in a very long time. He rested back on the pillows, watching them kiss through a hooded gaze. Feeling her shift positions so that his head fell into her lap. And he drifted off, satiated in body, but still feeling like he was missing something here.

And the discomfort of what it could be would certainly haunt his dreams.

~

Zara

Hux's head rested against Zara's stomach and she flexed her fingers through his tousled salt-and-pepper curls. He smiled in his sleep but didn't wake. She glanced up to find Richard watching, his dark eyes tracking every motion of her hand.

"Why is he so protective?" he said softly.

Her fingers faltered and she broke her gaze from Richard's for a moment. She explored Hux's face, that beautiful face she knew so well. Dark stubble highlighted his sharp jawline and his full lips were relaxed. He looked younger in that moment. More at ease. When she saw him like this, Richard's question took on a far more urgent nature. After all, Hux's normal tension *was* because he was always protecting her.

"You don't have to tell me," Richard added.

She drew a shaky breath. She had trusted this man with her body and he had proven to be a good steward. And even though she ought not, she wanted to trust him with something deeper. More meaningful. Consequences be damned.

"You know I was a courtesan," she began. "From the time I was eighteen until I was twenty-two. And *that* is when I met Hux."

Richard's brow wrinkled. "He was your protector?"

She shook her head slowly, gathering her emotions. Needing to because the past was flooding back and threatening to mob her. To stay grounded, she focused on Hux again. Hux's face. Only Hux. Her rock.

"No," she said when she could find her voice again. "He was a thief, just like he is now. He was doing what he does best when he stumbled upon me with my so-called protector at the time. The man was angry with me for something I didn't want to do and he had dragged me into a private space where no one could see. He struck me. When I tried to leave, he..." She trailed off as the lump in her throat cut off her ability to form words for a moment. "He took what I no longer freely offered. And then Hux burst into the room."

Richard's brows both went up and his expression softened with not pity, but empathy. Understanding. Grief on her behalf. "Zara...I'm so sorry."

She shrugged, but she knew her face revealed her pain. She'd never been able to school it when it came to this subject. How many times had she blamed herself for what had happened to her that night? How many times had she told Hux that if she had given consent once, perhaps she had no right to refuse it afterward.

And how many times had Hux dried her tears and gently reminded her that she was worthy of respect and care, whether she made her money on her back or any other way.

She gently tangled her fingers into Hux's hair again. "He carried me out of the gathering where I'd been attacked. He was a stranger, but I was so frightened and injured that I couldn't run. He felt...*safe*, and then he proved he was just that when took care of me that night, tending to my wounds. He did so the next and the next, never asking me for anything in return. Never demanding anything at all from me."

Richard looked down at him. "A gentleman in the truest sense of the word."

She smiled. "Never let him hear you call him that. He'd be offended."

"I'll keep it in mind." Richard chuckled despite the topic.

She sighed and returned to her story. "Eventually he asked if I'd be his partner. Over the next few months he taught me how to pick a pocket and a lock. He taught me signals so he'd know which man to swindle. We came up with dozens of scenarios and games over the years." She hesitated as she traced her fingertip across Hux's lips. Those lips that had spoken gentle words, had kissed away her tears, had brought her such pleasure so that the pain became a more and more distant memory. "And he reminded me how to laugh again."

"He became your lover."

Zara continued to stare at Hux as her heart swelled with all the emotion this handsome fallen angel brought out in her. "No. Not for over six months."

Richard's brow wrinkled in surprise. "But you have such intense chemistry."

"We do," she agreed with a little smile. "And I knew he wanted me. Once some of the shock of what had happened wore off, I knew I wanted him, too. But I wasn't ready."

"I can imagine not," Richard said.

She nodded. "He never pushed. He never asked for anything. After a few months, I confronted him about it, asked if he didn't find me attractive enough. I thought he'd shake the house down with his laughter. He told me that he wanted me more than anyone he'd ever met." She felt her cheeks heat with a blush. "But that I was the one who was in charge. That he would wait. He would agree to nothing more than our partnership if that's what I wanted. But that when I was ready, if I wanted him, he was...he was mine."

She struggled to say the last bit. She knew it was true, of course. Peregrine Huxley was hers. There was never any doubt of that. And yet they never spoke it. They never expressed the feelings that flowed between them as easily as the desire. He didn't push for that either, and she wasn't brave enough to be the one. Just in case.

"And one night you did," Richard pressed.

"Yes," she agreed. "One night I couldn't take it anymore. I slipped into his bed, and from that moment on we were lovers. But you've seen how he is. He never takes, only gives. He never pushes, only surrenders. He could have me any way he liked, but he is always careful. Like I'm glass."

"No," Richard said softly. "Like you are fine china. Like you are precious jewels."

Heat flooded her cheeks at that flowery description. One she didn't feel fit her. She shrugged. "One way or another, he is deeply protective."

"He seemed to like it when I was more dominant with you," Richard said. "After his initial worry was assuaged."

"He likes it when I come," she said.

Richard gave a half-smile and leaned in closer. "*I* like it when you come, Zara."

He kissed her and her fingers bunched against Hux's scalp as their tongues gently tangled. Then less gently. Richard cupped the back of her neck loosely, holding her against him with more of that dominance that she hadn't realized she so deeply craved.

"Are you two starting without me?" Hux asked, raising his head with a sleepy smile. "That seems very unfair."

Richard laughed and it broke their kiss. He shifted and tilted Hux's chin up, kissing him with just as much passion as he had kissed Zara. The emotions that had been there faded a little. He let them go, she allowed for it, too. Whatever confessions she'd made, or he'd made earlier were tucked away to be forgotten for a while.

"If it is unfair, then I suggest you do something about it," Richard said.

Hux groaned against the other man's lips and then gently shifted Zara to lie between them, facing Richard. The world began to melt as both their hands smoothed over her naked flesh and each other's, awakening her desire all over again, as if it hadn't been slaked so recently. And as she sank into the pleasure of it all, she pushed away the soft confessions she had made about her past with Hux. And the nagging sense of discomfort that perhaps she was going to lose something if she didn't change the dynamic between them.

CHAPTER 11

Richard

The next week passed in a blur. Richard woke every morning to the sight of these two remarkable people in his bed. Often with one or both of them teasing him to completion or giving each other pleasure while he watched or joined. They fucked in every room in his house, loudly enough that the servants stopped making eye contact. They also shared meals and laughs, walks in the countryside around his estate and picnics by the lake where they fished.

He shook the memories from his head as he sat up straighter at his desk and stretched his back. He'd left Zara and Hux upstairs an hour before, sleeping off another night of endless passion, and come down to catch up on some estate work he'd pushed from his mind during their stay. But now the books were balanced and the bills were paid, as well as Peyton's questions about some household matters answered. The butler was well-trained not to show emotion, but Richard had heard the lilt to his tone when he'd asked, "And how long will Mr. Huxley and Miss Cooper remain with us, sir?"

Richard hated that he didn't know the answer. None of them ever brought up their staying even though their agreed upon time together had passed already. To Richard's frustration none of them ever brought up *any* subject that was too deep. He had already made his confessions about his past and Zara hers. But Hux remained closed off, slightly separated, at least emotionally, from Richard. Did he give of his body? Oh yes. But his heart remained unreachable.

It frustrated Richard, but he could see there were moments when it *hurt* Zara. It was obvious that she longed for more, yet never reached for it. He could understand why, after what she'd been through, the life she'd led. But he was becoming very invested in her happiness. In her future.

He sighed and pushed to his feet. Perhaps it was time to stop being cowardly and simply speak to both of them about this. Peyton's question left an open door to press and see where they all stood. See where the future might lay.

He was about to exit his study when there was a light knock on the door and then Peyton reappeared. "I beg your pardon, sir, but you have a caller."

"A caller?" Richard repeated. "Who?"

Peyton handed over the card. It read, *Gilbert Wren, Investigator.* Richard's brow wrinkled. "An investigator?"

Peyton inclined his head. "So he says, sir. He implies he has questions for you about a case he is involved in. I might have simply sent him away as you have been...er...busy the past few days, but he seems the kind of man who cannot be deterred."

Richard came back around his desk and set the card down there. "Send him in. I'll manage him." He worried his lip as Peyton made his way out the door. "Peyton," he called out, and the butler turned. "Are Zara and Huxley up yet?"

"I do not know for certain, sir," Peyton said, again not revealing anything of his thoughts on the matter. "They do not often ring the bell for any of the servants. But I do believe

I heard them moving around in your chamber a short time ago."

Richard nodded. "Thank you. That will be all."

Peyton left to get his guest and Richard sat down at his desk, staring at the investigator's card yet again. He had a hard time believing that the man would be here over something Richard had done or seen. His life before Zara and Hux had been rather mundane. He had no enemies, he had witnessed no crimes.

But the two in his bed could certainly be the subject of an investigation. And a chill ran up his spine at that idea just as Peyton returned to his study, a tall, handsome man at his heels. A man with intelligent eyes that darted all around Richard's study before settling on him, pinning him.

"Mr. Wren, sir." Peyton inclined his head and left them.

Richard looked his new companion up and down. He did not rise, nor offer his hand in greeting before he said, "Good afternoon, Mr. Wren."

"Mr. Fitzroy," Wren said softly. "A pleasure to make your acquaintance."

"As it is yours," Richard said, and waved Wren to a chair across from his. Wren took it and leaned back, still observing in a most startling way. "I'm afraid I do not understand the purpose of your visit, sir. Your card says you are an investigator. Since we are not acquainted previously, one must assume you are here on some sort of official business. What are you investigating?"

"You are correct, sir. I do come to you in the capacity of my profession. As for my investigation, it is more about who I'm investigating rather than what." Wren held his gaze evenly. "And who I am investigating are Peregrine Huxley and Zara Cooper."

Hux

Hux and Zara came down the hallway together, his hand at her back, reveling in the warmth of her just as much when they walked as he had when he'd been buried balls deep in her flexing body not twenty minutes before. Being near her was the key pleasure of his life. And that was becoming a clearer and clearer reality in this house, with Richard involved.

Hux didn't know how to handle that. He'd kept everyone in his life at arm's length for such a long time. It was for protection of them as much as for himself. But now he felt the tug of longing toward her. Not for her body, but for her heart. For Richard's heart. It could only end in tears, he knew. After all, he had never belonged with people like them. He wasn't educated, he wasn't posh. He was a trifle, and he'd built walls around himself for a long time so that that fact wouldn't ever cause him pain.

But he ignored all that for now. For now they were simply coming down to find Richard. Perhaps they'd share a lazy, late meal and then go back to bed for more exploration of pleasure. Or they'd walk the grounds, hands tangling, laughter echoing, and he could pretend, if only for a while, that this was real, not some dreamy fantasy.

As they reached Richard's study door, Hux noted it was partly open. He heard voices from within. Richard's, which he knew so well now. But another man's, too. At first he thought it might be the butler, Peyton, but as they got closer, he could tell from the tone that it wasn't. It was someone who concerned Richard—Hux heard the strain in his voice.

He stopped, moving toward the wall as they came closer. He looked back and Zara and found she looked as concerned as he was. *Who is that?* she mouthed, nodding her head toward the study door.

He shook his head and lifted a finger to his lips, encouraging her silence. She rolled her eyes, a message to him that this wasn't the first time she'd snuck around eavesdropping on people. He smiled at her, despite his increasing concern, and then edged up to the door so he could listen.

"You are correct, sir. I do come to you in the capacity of my profession. As for my investigation, it is more about who I'm investigating rather than what," came the unknown voice from within. "And who I am investigating are Peregrine Huxley and Zara Cooper."

Zara's mouth dropped open and Hux's heart began to throb. An investigator. Looking for them. His first reaction, from his gut, was to grab Zara and run. Just run away, far away and never return to England. But when he looked at her, her eyes wide and sparkling with worry, he hated to think of taking her on a life on the run. Of seeing her worry every day, look over her shoulder at all times. Of knowing he had at last made her give up any hope of the kind of life she deserved.

Richard had been quiet after that statement but now he cleared his throat. Through the little gap between the wall and the door edge, Hux could see a glimpse of him, sitting at his desk. Richard's face was impassive, his hands folded on the desktop. "You said you are investigating two people. Regarding what exactly?"

"Theft," the investigator said evenly. "My employer attended a ball two weeks ago and had a valuable pocket watch stolen from his person. He suspects the two people I'm looking for and is determined to get the item back…as well as to bring the thieves to justice, as swiftly and severely as possible."

"A serious charge. But what does that have to do with me?" he asked, voice calm. Hux almost smiled. The man could be a professional grifter with such schooled responses and easy lies.

"There is a rumor that the pair may be staying here in your home," the investigator explained.

Richard's brows went up. "How scandalous a thought, Mr. Wren. But I fear it is only rumor. There were…friends staying with me, but they left two days ago now. A Mr. and Mrs. Valentine. They were heading to Wales, I believe, to see family and friends there."

There was a long silence. Hux couldn't see the other man's face, but he could read body language. Wren didn't believe Richard. Which meant Richard was now caught up in suspicion as well. And all because of Hux. Wasn't it all because of Hux? He had dragged Zara into his life, after all. He had done the same now with Richard.

His heart throbbed and he gripped his hands as fists at his sides as he waited for the investigator to respond. Wren slowly stood. "If that is the case, I must have bad information and I apologize for wasting your time."

He extended a hand and Richard shook it. "No apology necessary, Mr. Wren. What an excitement to think for a moment that I could be involved in something so shocking. My life is rather boring otherwise."

"Hmmm." Wren tilted his head and now Hux caught a glimpse of a harsh jawline, tight with disbelief. "Mr. Fitzroy, I have no reason to doubt you. From all my research, you are known as an upstanding person. But if you do know these people or are harboring them in some way, please realize that those who hired me are bent on destruction. They won't stop. You have my card. It has my direction at the inn in the village. I'll be there for a few days at least while I investigate any other leads on the matter. If you think of anything that you left out, please do contact me."

"Of course."

They were wrapping up now, and Hux grabbed Zara's arm and tugged her into a nearby parlor. They stood behind the door, listening as Richard escorted Wren to the foyer. Their voices echoed, mindless small talk about the weather and the roads and then the front door closed.

Hux released Zara at last and she crossed to the settee, sinking into the cushions and covering her face with her hands. He stared at her, her shoulders rolled forward in defeat and pain and fear. And he hated himself even more intensely.

He cleared his throat and stepped into the hallway as Richard made his way back in long, steady strides. When he saw Hux, his eyes went wide. They stared at each other a moment, Hux trying to memorize every line of his face. Then Richard shook his head. "You heard?"

Hux jerked out an unsteady nod. "Yes," he whispered, and motioned behind him into the room. "We both did."

Richard's mouth tightened and he drew an unsteady breath. "Then we have a great deal to talk about."

Hux felt his jaw tighten as together they walked into the parlor. Zara lifted her head as they did so, her expression drawn and filled with pain and fear. It hit Hux in the chest, increasing his already pulsing guilt.

Richard crossed to her and sat beside her, gathering her into his arms and offering the comfort that Hux couldn't. He stared at them, drinking them in. If there was an investigation, it was very likely that he would be torn away from them, whether because he had to run or because he was taken.

And in that moment, he felt the absolute devastation of that idea. Of losing them. These two people he cared for...loved. Loved, could he love them? With Zara it had been constant building emotion for so long, which he tried to ignore even though it was part of him down to his very core.

Richard was more surprising. Hux didn't let people in, not so quickly. But he felt such a connection to this man. Such a powerful drive to be near him and know him and give whatever he needed.

What if what they needed was for him to step away? To protect her? To protect him?

He cleared his throat. His voice caught as he said, "If I...if I turned myself in to this man..."

Zara shoved from Richard's arms and was on her feet immediately. She stepped toward Hux. "No!"

He shook his head. "Zara, listen to me, we've talked about this many times over the years, you know what is best. If I told him I was the only one involved in any scheme—"

She moved into his space and pressed her hands against his chest, pushing him back like she could move him away from the idea. "No!" she repeated, louder and wilder.

Richard got up slowly. "He's trying to protect you, Zara."

"I bloody well know that," she said, pivoting toward him, then back to Hux. "You have spent years trying to protect me. But I will not let you do this! I won't let you sacrifice yourself for me. Not for me, Huxley. I would not survive without you."

He glanced toward Richard. "Perhaps you wouldn't have to be alone."

Her eyes went wide and she stared at him, unblinking. Then she shook her head. "Fuck you, Huxley. It isn't about needing a man at my side. It's about *you*, you great oaf."

She turned on her heel and stomped from the room, but not before Hux saw her tears begin to fall. He bent his head.

"You aren't going to follow her?" Richard asked softly.

Hux turned to him. "Perhaps she needs to be angry with me. Perhaps she needs to hate me."

Richard let out a long sigh. "You'll protect her to the end."

"I would protect her to my dying breath if I had to," Hux snapped. He sat down hard on the settee she had abandoned and scrubbed a hand over his face. "What do you think of this man, this investigator?"

"Hard to say, I only spoke to him for a moment. He was hard to read."

Hux arched a brow. "Fitzroy."

Richard ducked his head. "I think he is a resolute person who likely takes his duties seriously. He has been paid, probably handsomely, to find you both. I doubt he'll stop until he has something to report to the person who hired him."

Huxley shook his head as the truth sank in. The future laid itself out in front of him and there was nothing good about it. He sighed. "I...I have always been reckless. Danced along the edge of ruination. Sometimes that was the only thing that made me feel alive."

Richard's brow wrinkled and he stepped closer but didn't join Hux on the settee or touch him. As if he knew Hux needed the space still. "Why?" he asked.

Hux stared at the flames dancing in the fire. There had been confessions between them before now. Richard about his late wife. He knew Zara had told Richard her history. But he had remained silent, not wanting to risk vulnerability. But now that he was on the cusp of losing everything, it seemed vulnerability was the only path.

"My mother was a lightskirt before she met my stepfather. He got her hired on as a cook," he said softly. "But he was a cruel drunk who would never let her forget what she was and how he judged her for it. I would have done anything to escape their house and their violence. When she killed him..." His voice caught.

Richard did sit next to him now, his hand coming to cover Hux's. The warmth and weight of it was so comforting. He wanted to sink into him like he'd watched Zara do a moment before. To give him everything and anything if it meant he wouldn't lose him. Lose her.

But that wasn't possible now.

"She killed him," he continued slowly. "A clear case of self-defense. But there was an investigation and she didn't intend to stay for it. She ran. She left me behind and she ran."

Richard let out a sharp breath. "How old were you?"

"Nine," Hux admitted.

"Hux," Richard whispered. "What did you do? Did you have family to turn to?"

Hux smiled at him even though there was no pleasure to this, no warmth or humor. "You really are almost an innocent to the ways of the real world, aren't you? There was no one. So I scrapped. I was always good at scrapping. At surviving. I learned how to pickpocket and steal and please enough to get close so I could strike. I learned to seduce and play and lie. And I liked it. I *like* knowing I could come to the edge of destruction and control it enough to stay on the right side."

Richard nodded, and it was like he...understood. Not possible considering how far apart their lives had been. No two men could have been more different in their original circumstances. And yet he felt no judgment from Richard. Nothing but acceptance, the same kind he always felt from Zara.

"It was fine to be that way when it was just me," he continued. "But I never should have continued on once Zara came into my life. Once I took responsibility for her well-being, I never should have been...been me." He said it and it was like he'd burned a little part of himself away.

"She would not want you to be anyone else but you," Richard said. "You *know* that. You must feel it when she looks at you as she does."

Hux bent his head. He did know it. It only made it worse.

"But I'm not worthy of what she is. What she could be. If I were gone—" he had to stop and take a deep breath. "If I were gone, either by arrest or escape, would you take care of her?"

Richard made a strangled sound in his throat, and for a moment Hux thought he would argue. But instead he whispered, "I would protect her, yes. I would take care of her."

"Would you marry her?" Hux asked. Richard stared at him, eyes wide. "Don't look at me that way. You know that a man of your influence could protect her from my consequences if she were your wife."

"I would marry her if she would allow it," Richard finally said, and there was a firmness to his tone. A determination. "Whatever else happened, I wouldn't let her ever come to harm."

Relief mixed with grief and they flooded Hux's system until his eyes stung with tears. "Good," he said softly. "Good that will make whatever comes next easier."

He moved to stand, but Richard kept his hand on his wrist and held him steady. "And who will protect you, Huxley?"

CHAPTER 12

Hux

Hux froze. The question burned and flowered and spread throughout his entire being because it meant so much. He forced himself to meet Richard's gaze. It seemed this man wished to stand in the way of what must be done as much as Zara did. Which meant Hux had to force him away, just as he was trying to do with her. He couldn't let them burn in the fire he had set and would potentially destroy him now.

"I don't need protection," he said. "Not from you."

He meant it to sting. Richard didn't even flinch. "Don't do that, Hux. Don't pretend to be stone when I know full well that you are flesh and blood, a beating heart, a decent soul."

Hux turned his head. "Stop."

Richard caught his chin, his fingers stroking lightly as he forced him back to look at him. "I won't. You know you can't stop me. Or her, likely. Just because you spent your life not protected doesn't mean you don't deserve it. That you don't have two people in your life that will do *everything* to provide it. *I* will do everything to provide it, Huxley. Because I won't lose you."

Hux stared at him, shocked at what he was offering. Bewitched by the idea of it, at least momentarily. But then reality returned. "You will not dash yourself on the rocks for me, I won't let you."

Richard's expression softened. "And you say *I'm* the innocent. You think this is all or nothing. Destruction for all or only for one. I adore you, Hux, but you are wrong. There are a thousand hues between black and white. And I can see a dozen ways to end this without you being destroyed, her being destroyed. Without you being lost."

A swell of hope filled Hux's chest, but he pushed it away with all his might. Hope was never a good thing. Hope could lead to disappointment and damage. He would not entertain it.

"And why would you do that?" he asked, sharp. "This was a lark, Fitzroy."

To his surprise, Richard leaned forward and kissed him, silencing his words. Hux sank into it for a moment, reveling in his taste, in the pressure of his mouth. But then he shook off that reaction.

"No," Hux insisted. "It's a game."

Now Richard caught his lapels and yanked him harder against him, his mouth more insistent. Huxley felt like he was sinking into warm bathwater and he never wanted to leave. His voice was much weaker when he murmured, "You are a trifle to me."

Richard dug his fingers into Hux's hair and tilted his head. Hux couldn't resist any longer. His mouth opened and suddenly there were no more words or denials. There was only this connection. There was only this man.

There was only their desire that was so tied to their feelings. Hux wanted that desire, even if he kept telling himself it would be one of the last times he could allow it.

He didn't resist as Richard lowered him to the cushions. As he covered him, letting Hux feel his weight. Hux's arms came around his back and he made a muffled sound of surrender. He felt

Richard smile against his mouth and then the kiss deepened even further.

He dragged his hands down Richard's back, feeling the firm muscle through his jacket. He cupped his backside and Richard flexed against him with a grunt, their hard cocks rubbing briefly as they rose and fell against each other.

By God, did he want this man. He wanted to feel him shudder around his cock. He wanted to watch him arch with pleasure as he spent. Nothing else mattered in that moment because everything else was too dire and terrifying.

He focused on Richard, grinding him harder against himself as their kiss grew wild and wicked and animal. At last they broke away and Hux panted up at him, "Let me."

Richard nodded without hesitation. As if giving himself was easy. His body, his soul, his everything. Hux hated him and adored him for that in equal measure. He reversed their positions, shifting to perch between Richard's legs. He ran his hands down Richard's body, once again memorizing every line. He didn't want to forget even one of them later. Later...

He cut the dire thought off again and let his fingers drag down Richard's stomach. He unfastened his coat, let his hands move down the placard of his trousers. Felt the strain of Richard's cock growing more insistent with each glancing touch of Hux's fingers. Richard strained upward, making a demand with his hips.

Hux couldn't deny it. He lowered the placard and caught Richard's cock, stroking him once, twice, feeling his blood rise in response. Then Hux met those startling blue eyes of his and held there as he lowered his mouth to Richard. As he closed around him, taking him deep into his throat, Richard moaned. God, he loved that sound. Loved that feeling of this man inside of him. Loved the taste of him.

He was going to lose...

No. He sucked harder to make the thought go away, and Richard jolted. "Hux," he grunted, his fingers coming into his hair.

He was like Zara that way, always tangling his fingers in the curls, demanding more.

He gave it, taking and taking, giving and giving until Richard was trembling, his head thrashing on the pillows. He sat up on his elbows, lifting his hips in time to Hux's mouth even as he groaned out, "Fuck me."

Hux stopped his movements and stared at Richard. They had done so much in their time together, but when it came to sex between them, Hux was always the one being taken.

But right now the thought of burying himself in this man was almost maddening. It made him weak and achy and needy in a new and powerful way. He would not deny himself this, because so much would be denied so soon.

"Roll over," he ordered, hearing how rough his voice was. How hard.

Richard leaned up and kissed him, slow and soft, and then did as he'd been told, shoving his trousers down around his knees as he did so. Hux flipped up the long length of his shirt tails and jacket, peering down at the gorgeous arse before him. He leaned in and lightly licked, and Richard hissed in pleasure.

"Please," he moaned.

God, but he loved to make him beg. With Zara he'd always been so careful, and watching Richard dominate her more was thrilling, especially since she seemed to respond. But Hux was always hesitant. He needed to be her safe place.

But with Richard he felt no such drive. Only the drive to claim. He pulled out his cock and rubbed it against the entrance. Richard wasn't ready yet, but he wanted him to feel the pulse of what was going to happen, he wanted the heady rush of their bodies rubbing together.

"Fuck," Richard grunted and pushed back, taking just a tiny portion of what Hux could offer.

"You're going to hurt yourself," Hux whispered, pulling back. "You're not ready."

"Make me ready then," Richard whimpered, clutching at the arm of the settee with both hands. "And do it. I need to feel you."

Hux didn't argue. He didn't tease anymore. He needed to feel this too. To erase some of the ugly with something beautiful. He spit against Richard's arse, rubbing the fluid in, stretching him slightly to ready him. He spit in his own palm, stroking his cock. This wasn't the most optimal way to do this, to ease the way, but it would do when things were so desperate.

When they were both wet, he pressed against him again, squeezing his eyes shut as he pushed forward into delicious heat, into tightness that made him go mad, into a gripping channel. Richard's cry of pleasure made Hux go weak and he gripped the other man's hips hard enough to bruise as almost unbearable sensation streaked through his entire body.

He fucked then. Hard and fast, grinding and groping and claiming like nothing else mattered. Richard met him stroke for stroke, just as wild and wanton for this as Hux was.

"I want to feel how hard you are," Hux whispered, wrapping his arm around Richard's stomach, gliding down to find the hard cock curled against his stomach. "Come for me."

As he said it, he began to stroke in time to his thrusts. Richard was gasping and groaning now, his thighs shaking, his arms straining. "Hux!" he jolted out at last as he came against Hux's palm.

The pleasure was too much. Hux joined him, pumping into him, filling him as he filled himself with all the connection and love and hope that he knew couldn't last. Wouldn't last because of what he was, who he was.

He collapsed over Richard, pressing kisses behind his ear, still stroking his twitching cock as they piled together on the settee. How long that lasted, Hux didn't know. Not long enough. At last Richard shifted beneath him, rolled to be under him again. Only this time they were nose to nose, face to face.

"I'm not going to lose you," he said.

Hux groaned and rested his head down on Richard's shoulder, breathing in his scent before he said, "Letting me fuck you isn't going to suddenly change my mind on this subject."

"Being fucked by you isn't going to change mine," Richard said with just as much strength and conviction. "Let me up."

Hux sighed and sat up, granting Richard the space to get to his feet. He readjusted, dressing himself swiftly. Hux remained as and where he was, just staring up at Richard.

"I'm going to get Zara," Richard explained. "Because this is not a conversation for you and me. It's for all of us. But while I'm gone, I want you to think about something."

"What?" Hux asked.

"Is it protecting her to take her heart from her chest? Is it protecting me?"

Hux bent his head. "It's not your hearts I'm worried about. It's the breath from your lungs. The life from your bodies."

Richard tilted his face up and shook his head. "My darling, we are talking about the same thing." He walked out of the room, leaving Hux to rest his head on the back of the settee with a loud sigh.

Fuck, but the man was determined to wear him down. Worse, it might work. And then where would they all be?

Nowhere good.

$\sim$

Zara

There were only a few times in Zara's life where she had cried until she felt there were no tears left in the world. This was one of them. She lay on her side in Richard's bed, her cheeks wet from them, her body weak from sobbing. She stared into nothingness and felt the tug of her future. There would be nothingness without Hux, too. He just didn't care enough to hear it. To understand that tearing himself away wasn't protection, it was torture.

She sat up, smoothing her hair and wiping her eyes. Part of her wanted to stay hidden in this warm room. To pretend that none of this was happening. To hide because surely Hux wouldn't leave without telling her goodbye.

Would he?

There was a light knock on the door, and Zara got to her feet as it opened. She tensed, readying for Hux...but it wasn't him. It was Richard who entered. A slightly tousled Richard, with a serious expression on his face.

And her knees nearly went out from under her. "He left," she said.

"No." Richard rushed to her, holding her up just as he had in the parlor when the investigator's interest had first been revealed.

Relief flowed through her and she rested her head on his shoulder. She smelled Hux on him and she breathed the scent in. Richard's hand came up to smooth her hair and he said, "Come back down with me, Zara. We'll talk to him together."

She lifted her head. "And what if we can't convince him?"

A little smile tilted Richard's lips. "Then we'll tie him up in the attic until we can save him."

That image elicited a laugh from her, even though she was still tense with fear and worry. Hux would be furious to be held captive, even for his own good. And yet she would risk his wrath, even his hatred, if she could save him.

"*I'll* talk to him," she said with a sigh. "As long as you stand by with the rope."

Richard wiped a tear from her cheek with his thumb and then leaned forward. His mouth was warm against hers, gentle. Soothing. When they parted, he took her arm and together they walked from the room, down the main stair and back into the parlor.

Hux was sprawled on the settee, just as mussed as Richard

looked, and she rolled her eyes. It seemed Richard had tried passion to convince him. It didn't look like it had worked.

Hux got up as she came closer. He stared at her like he was seeing her for the first time, and she released Richard and moved to him. She wrapped her arms around him, and for what seemed like an eternity, they just held each other. There were no words. No words were needed. She just felt him and his heartbeat and it made her feel safe.

At least for the time being. But at last he leaned back. "Zara," he began.

"If you are going to say anything after my name that involves you leaving me, then you can save your breath," Zara said.

Hux cupped her cheeks. "You have to let me go," he whispered, his breath warm on her lips. "I was never forever for you."

"That is shite and you know it," she snapped. "Why in the world would you think that?"

"Because you are lovely and intelligent and suited for far above a station than mine. When you were broken and bruised, I know it was helpful to come down to where I live, who I am, and never expect more. But you were always more and I always knew that one day you would remember that."

Her heart throbbed at that complete dismissal of what he had been to her. And her sudden understanding of how he viewed himself...why he never let her too close. She knew about his life, his past. It had taken years to hear it, to ease it out of him, but this man had suffered greatly. And it broke her heart to know he felt unworthy of her when in truth he was the person she admired and needed most in this world.

"Hux," she whispered.

He shook his head, still determined. "I was a time for you, but perhaps he..." He looked at Richard over her shoulder. "...is your future."

She tugged away from him, recoiling once more. "No," she said. "What part of no don't you understand? I won't leave you."

"Because you love him."

Richard said those words, quietly and calmly from behind her. Zara nearly stumbled hearing them. Things she had felt but feared to say because of the past. *Because* of what she knew about who Hux was and what he'd been through. Because if he didn't love her back it would destroy her.

But losing him would do that too. And perhaps her fear had been her greatest failing.

She drew a deep breath and met Hux's eyes. Lost herself in him for a moment, just as she wished to do for the rest of her life. "Because I love you," she repeated. "I love you, Peregrine Huxley."

If she hoped that confession would bring joy to his handsome face, it elicited the opposite response. Hux's expression crumpled and he moved away from her, pacing to the nearly chair and leaning heavily against its back with both hands.

"Don't love me, Zara," he murmured at last. "Not now. Not when you could be with someone who—"

He cut himself off and Zara realized in that moment that he wasn't about to make some excuse about the danger he was in due to the investigation. This denial was about that, yes, but also something deeper.

"What?" she demanded. "Respect me enough to finish the sentence, Hux."

He lifted his chin, defiant and beautiful, even as he made his face hard. "You could be with someone who makes this so easy."

Her mouth dropped open. Was *that* what he saw when he looked at her with Richard? That it was easy after such a struggle in their beginning? Did he see how she surrendered to this other man and decide that meant she wanted him more? That she could give something Hux couldn't take?

She moved toward him, long certain steps. He gripped the chair back even harder, his knuckles going white, but he didn't recoil. He didn't move away.

"If it is easy with Richard, it is because of you."

Hux's expression became confused and he shook his head. "I don't...I don't know what that means."

"You gave me my strength back. You protected me. *You.* Everything is because of you. Yes, I can give something to Richard, I can enjoy what he offers without fear or struggle. But that is because *you* taught me to trust myself again. And it doesn't hurt that I know you would tear limb from limb any man who ever hurt me."

"I would," he whispered.

They held stares for a long, charged moment and even though he hadn't said he loved her, she saw it in his warm eyes. She felt it in every fiber of this man who stood before her. She smiled because she couldn't help but do so. "Everything you are is what I want, not some idealized fairytale you imagined me living without you. And if you think I would lose you, you are a fool. I'm not going to lose you, Hux. *Ever.*"

"Neither am I." Richard moved to stand beside her and she linked her arm through his. Now they were a united front. Richard took a shaky breath. "I didn't love my wife, not enough. Because of the arranged marriage, I didn't give myself entirely. I suppose I feared that a part of me"—he reached out and touched Hux's cheek with the back of his hand—"would die," he finished. "And when she was gone, I punished myself for the times I wanted to be free."

Hux's face twisted with pain on Richard's behalf.

"I don't want regrets when it comes to you two," Richard continued. "You've both come to mean too much to me in such a short time."

"You two are relentless," Hux said with a shaky laugh. "And determined to save me, which I admit is a rather...odd feeling."

"Does that mean you'll allow us to try?" Zara asked, breathless as she waited his response. "Or at least you'll listen to Richard's plans?"

He touched her face, so gentle as he had always been gentle

with her. "Yes," he murmured. "Tell me what you think you can do."

Zara shut her eyes and gulped back a cry of relief. This was a first step, but not the end. If Richard didn't convince him, he might still run.

Richard seemed to understand that just as much. He nodded, suddenly very serious. "My entire life I have watched people with power leverage it for their own selfish needs. I've seen them damage and wound to get what they want and with very little consequence." He pursed his lips as if in disgust. "I've tried never to do the same. But now I think I shall leverage my position for the first time. To protect you."

Zara tilted her head. "You think you could?"

"The pocket watch you stole, was it from Bernard Varrick?"

She stared. "I think that was his name—how did you know that?"

"Well, I watched it bounce between your remarkable breasts when I caught you two fucking in the parlor at the ball," Richard reminded her. "And I recognized it. Varrick was constantly making mountains out of that thing. Flashing it around as some symbol of power or money."

Richard walked away, stroking his chin. "The truth is, Varrick is a silly man with very little power of his own. That watch was his grandfather's, given to him by his father. He's terrified of his father. It may be that he is trying to hide the robbery from him until he can crow that he's caught the culprits, hoping to stay the old man's wrath."

"An interesting tidbit of information, but what do you suggest with do with it?" Hux asked.

"Do you still have the piece?"

Hux exchanged a quick glance with Zara. "Yes," he said. "We hadn't the time to fence it after the ball. We were preparing to come here to your home. It's tucked away in a safe place in our room."

"Excellent. This investigator, Wren, while I do think he is a resolute person, I doubt he has any love lost for his bastard of a client. He must have noticed Varrick is a complete fool. He pursues you because he was hired to do a duty. I would wager he could be bargained with. Perhaps even bribed. Threatened, if it comes down to it. Especially if I could deliver what was lost to be returned to his employer."

Zara pivoted on Hux, hope blooming in her chest. "It's worth a try, isn't it?" she asked.

Hux pondered that question a moment and then looked at Richard. "If you go, bringing the watch with you, it could open you up to questions."

Richard nodded slowly. "Yes."

"Then I want to come too."

"Hux!" Zara said.

"That rather defeats the purpose of protecting you, my love," Richard said.

Zara caught her breath at how easily Richard threw out that term of endearment. And at how Hux's face lit up when he heard it. Oh yes, if they could push past this terrible bump, their road together could be so very happy.

"Then I won't come as me. I doubt the investigator knows what I look like to any great detail, but even if he does, my beard is grown out since the ball, we can smooth my hair. I'll become your solicitor, Mr. Northern, come with you to represent you in the return of the watch."

"Well, if you two are going, then I'm coming too," Zara said.

Richard let out a long sigh. "And just how will we explain *your* presence?"

Zara snorted and smiled up at Hux. "I've dressed as a man before."

"She's a very attractive young man, indeed," Hux said, reaching around to caress her backside.

Zara laughed and swatted at his hand even though she loved the weight of it. "I could be a footman. We'll make it work."

Richard stared at them. "It seems we have decided that we are a team. All for one and one for all, isn't that the line?"

"Oh Lord, don't quote Shakespeare to me," Hux grunted.

"And he thinks he's uncultured," Richard replied with a laugh.

"We're *more* than a team," Zara whispered as she took each of their hands. "We are each other's future."

Hux's smile fluttered, but he still looked uncertain. "First we have to resolve the past, but I promise you, when we have, I'll discuss a future."

She lifted up on her tiptoes and kissed him gently. "That's fair."

"So," Hux said, turning his attention to Richard. "How do you suggest we do this? And how soon can it be done?"

Richard nodded. "I have thoughts about that. Let's put our heads together and work out the details."

CHAPTER 13

Hux

Hux fought not to run a hand though his hair and cause his highly identifiable curls to come free of all the work Zara had done to smooth them earlier in the day. He was nervous as he paced Richard's study, waiting for the arrival of the investigator, Mr. Wren.

"Huxley," Zara said, reaching out to catch his hand as he passed by her. She looked up at him and squeezed. She was dressed in the livery of Richard's servants, her hair twisted and tucked and mostly hidden except for a rather thick queue that did little to hide its length. She looked like a very pretty young man. Hopefully Mr. Wren would not look too closely at her.

Richard sat at his desk. "Pacing won't help."

Hux snorted out a humorless laugh. "It doesn't hurt."

"Then by all means continue," Richard said with a chuckle. "Your backside looks quite fine from several angles when you do it, and I'm sure I can replace the carpet after you wear a path through it."

Hux glared at him playfully and would have continued on his

way, but there was a light rap at the door. Zara leapt up and moved to it, straightening her spine as she tried to get into the character of a servant, here to standby in case they needed anything in the course of your business.

Hux stepped to the desk and smoothed his jacket, testing at the pocket watch was inside for the transfer of the item. God, he hoped this went well. In the day since they'd come up with this plan, he had found himself daring to picture a life with the two remarkable people in this room.

Perhaps that was foolish since he could lose it. But it felt so damned good.

He blinked as Richard nodded to Zara and she took a place at the sideboard, pouring tea for everyone as the butler opened the door. "Mr. Wren to see you, Mr. Fitzroy."

Richard inclined his head and Peyton stepped aside to reveal the investigator. Hux observed him in one quick sweep, taking in all the information he could. He was a handsome devil, that was undeniable. With a thick mop of dark hair, dark blue eyes and a nose that looked like it might have been broken a time or two over the course of...Hux would wager about thirty years. He appeared to be a serious person, and an observant one, for he felt himself being sized up just as he was doing the same.

Richard must have felt it too because he came around the desk, hand extended and partially blocked Hux. "Mr. Wren, thank you for returning. I hope I didn't take you away from anything pressing."

Wren inclined his head, his attention now focused on Richard. "My pressing matter remains the same, Mr. Fitzroy. It sounded as though you might have more information for me. Perhaps something you recalled after our discussion yesterday."

Richard gave a flutter of a smile. Not his real one that Hux knew so well. Loved to coax. This was a game. "You are a singularly minded person, I respect that. Please, come sit. Will you have tea? My footman will oblige."

Wren glanced toward Zara, but he didn't take her in with the same intensity that he had Hux, to Hux's great relief. "No, thank you. I appreciate the offer, but I'd rather get to the matter at hand."

"Of course," Richard said. "Stand by, would you? In case we require anything." Zara inclined her head and stepped back, worrying her hands a moment before she remembered herself and put them behind her back. Richard returned to his place at the desk and motioned toward Hux. "This is my solicitor, Mr. Northern."

"Mr. Wren," Hux said softly, making eye contact. Ducking it would only draw more attention to it. He wanted Wren to think he was exactly who he claimed.

"Mr. Northern," Wren said slowly before he returned his gaze to Richard. "If you have brought along a witness, I assume you have much more to say than perhaps I realized. Please, do tell."

Richard nodded. "I think we need to be honest with each other, sir. Your client is Bernard Varrick."

Wren's brow arched. "It is. I wonder how you know that."

Hux tensed. This was the risk now and while he liked taking it for himself, watching Richard dance along the edge of destruction was far less entertaining. But he did well, he didn't even acknowledge the statement and kept going.

"What if I could return the missing pocket watch to Mr. Varrick—through you, of course—and end this entire situation?"

Wren held his gaze for a beat, two. He slightly shifted in his place. "You have the watch."

"If I did, would returning it resolve the matter without further incident?"

Wren stared at Richard evenly for what felt like a very long time. At last he said, "I was hired not only to find the watch, Mr. Fitzroy. Mr. Varrick demands justice for the people who took it."

Richard's jaw clenched. "Mr. Varrick is a spoiled man-child

who is more afraid of his father's wrath than he cares about true justice in any way."

Hux held his breath. Wren's cheek twitched like he wanted to smile, the only indication that he found humor in that statement. But it gave Hux hope.

"You may not be wrong," the investigator said slowly. "Though it isn't my place to judge the value of my clientele. I would not wish for that to be my reputation."

"Why would it be?" Richard asked. "No one would know about it but you and me. You would return to your client with his missing item and tell him that the perpetrators have fled to the continent. Knowing the man as well as I do, I assume he will be so pleased not to have to tell his father what happened to a priceless family heirloom that he will not think one more moment about who caused his very brief pain."

Wren continued to look at Richard, reading him, Hux could see. Coming up with answers to questions that were dangerous to ask. Hux wanted so desperately to intervene, but when he glanced over at Zara at the door, she quickly shook her head. And he knew she was right. There was no reason for him to reveal his true identity at this point.

It would only make things worse.

"I would also make it worth your trouble by matching whatever it is that Mr. Varrick has paid you for your services."

"Two-hundred and fifty pounds?" Wren said. "You'd be willing to pay two-hundred and fifty pounds to return a watch that you didn't steal just so the perpetrators were not pursued?"

Hux's stomach turned. That was no small sum. More than the income of many a person for an entire year in his world.

"Would it be agreeable to you?" Richard asked softly.

"May I see the watch?" Wren asked.

"Of course." Richard motioned to Hux, and he had to force himself to come forward. He reached into his pocket and withdrew the silk square they had wrapped the piece in. He set it on the desk in front of Wren and gently folded the fabric back so that the watch was revealed.

Wren glanced up at him, gaze narrowed briefly and then picked up the watch. He weighed it in his hand, drew out a magnifying glass to examine the diamonds more closely, opened it and looked inside at the watch face and engraving. At last, he set it back into the silk and folded his arms.

"It does appear to be the correct item," he said. "And I'm sure Mr. Varrick will be pleased to have it. I agree to your terms, Mr. Fitzroy. I see no reason to pursue anyone regarding this matter."

Hux steadied himself on the edge of the desk as relief washed through him. He saw Zara do the same before she straightened back up in the guise of servant. Wren looked up at Hux, then back at Richard. "Will you answer a question?" he asked.

Richard nodded. "I will try."

"You must care very deeply for your...*friends*...if you are willing to risk yourself. To make yourself part of a crime. Are they worth it?"

Richard swallowed hard and there was no hesitation on his face as he said, "They are worth a great deal more, Mr. Wren."

Wren drew in a long breath, and for a moment Hux saw emotion flutter across the man's face. Like he understood the dynamics in some odd way. Like he felt them from the inside. But then he pushed to his feet, sweeping up the watch as he did so and tucking it into his inside pocket.

"I hope they are grateful," he said. "I shall return this forthwith and with as few details as possible."

"Excellent," Richard said. "I'll be certain the money is at your office in London before week's end."

Wren extended a hand and the two men shook before Richard motioned to the door and followed him out to escort him to the foyer. When they were gone, Zara rushed across the room and bounded into Hux's arms. She didn't speak, just lifted her mouth to his, kissing him with relief and passion and love. He drank her in, cupping her backside as she wrapped her legs around him and held tight.

He laughed as she drew back and stared at him, like she was trying to memorize his face. "I rather like you in trousers, my dear."

"I'll wear them every day if it makes you happy after this. After I almost lost you," she said.

As Richard returned to the room, Hux let out a shaky sigh. He set Zara down and she moved to Richard to kiss him. "I can't believe that worked."

"He seemed a reasonable man," Richard said with a shrug. "And so I hoped reason...and a bit of a bribe...would satisfy him."

"Will it satisfy Varrick?" Hux asked.

"Varrick is a fool," Richard said. "But he's a man intent on protecting his reputation. If the watch is back in his possession, I very much doubt he'll want to revisit the matter. You are safe, Hux. You and Zara are free."

Hux nodded. "Because of you."

"And that means that future you promised to consider is right in front of you, my love," Zara said, taking his hand, lifting it to her lips. "It's right here."

He bent his head. "Love is a risk," he said softly.

"And you like risks." Zara smiled.

"I meant a risk for you two. A risk to love me."

Her expression relaxed and she cupped his cheeks. "You are the surest wager I ever made in my life, Huxley. Never a risk. Never."

He looked at her, looked Richard beside her. He couldn't help but picture a life with them. One of passion, yes, but also affection. Of friendship and love. Of learning each other, growing together. A life worth living. Worth risking for.

"I love you, Zara," he whispered. Her smile faltered and tears filled her eyes at that confession. His too, if he were honest with himself. It felt good to say that to her. Right. "I have loved you for so long that I can't imagine my life without you. How to unbind the parts of us that make us whole together."

"Luckily you don't have to know," Zara said. "Because I love you too."

Hux looked at Richard then, who was watching them with what seemed to be undiluted pleasure. "And as for you..." he said.

Richard nodded. "As for me."

"The intensity of what I feel when I'm near you is...intoxicating, overpowering, shocking sometimes. And I've never experienced anything like it. I feel it grow with every moment we're together. And I know that is love. Love that will blossom and grow with time together."

"Yes," Zara agreed. "It's the same for me, Richard. I would not want to be without you. If you'll have us."

Richard laughed, his smile so bright and beautiful that it was almost blinding. And yet Hux stared straight into it because it was his. And hers. And theirs. "I would have you both. For the rest of my days. I would love you both and take care of you both. Joyfully."

They moved together then, all at once until they were in each other's arms. Holding each other, kissing each other, declaring with bodies what they had declared with their words and accepted with their hearts.

That love would win. Forever.

EPILOGUE

One year later

Zara

The ballroom was bustling as Zara moved through the crowd, smiling at people she vaguely knew, batting her eyes at gentlemen who would love to get closer. She wasn't sure who her mark was tonight, but she did know, as she found Richard and Hux across the room, standing close together at the edge of the dancefloor, that whatever happened tonight, it would be enjoyable.

She stopped for a moment, just drinking in the sight of them together. Most people here wouldn't notice the way they slightly leaned toward each other, wouldn't recognize the adoration in Hux's eyes when Richard smiled up at him. They hid in plain sight, something she and Hux had become well-versed at during their years as thieves. A game Richard played just as well now that they were all lovers and loves.

She adored their bond. Hers with both men and also theirs to each other. In the year since Richard had saved Hux and they had pledged themselves to each other, body and soul, Hux had become more open. Happier. She was, too. Being finally settled, complete, would do that to a woman.

As if he sensed her regard, Hux glanced across the room at her and arched a brow before he crooked his finger at his hip and secretly beckoned her to him. She went, as she would always go when he called. His little puppet very happily on his string until she took her dying breath.

As she reached them, she barely resisted the urge to kiss first one then the other. Not here. Not yet. "And here are the two most irresistible men in England," she said with a smile for them. "Do you have something to tell me?"

Richard let his gloved fingers slid forward and he briefly touched the inside of her wrist. Not something almost anyone else in the room would ever notice, but enough that she was set aflame. The desire never seemed to cease.

"See the gentleman there standing next to the punch bowl?" Richard asked.

She glanced over to see who he meant and shuddered. "The popinjay with the ridiculously oiled hair?"

Richard nodded. "Just the one. That is the third son of the Earl of Gillroy. Rich, pompous, abusive toward the servants."

"You do find us the best toys, Richard," Hux said softly, close to Richard's ear so that he shivered with pleasure. "It's always more fun to rob a bastard who deserves what he gets. We should have caught you up as our spy years ago."

Richard chuckled. "Just remember that I'm your favorite play-thing, Huxley."

Their easy teasing made her smile, but it fell as Zara examined the bastard who was their mark. "If he's an abusive twat, then I don't think he deserves those lovely bejeweled cufflinks," she murmured. "Huxley, are you ready?"

"For you? For him?" Hux smiled slightly. "For this? Always. Lead the way, my love. And I'll be right behind you."

She grinned at the pair before she weaved her way toward a gentleman whose night she would revel in ruining. And after? Well, afterward, she would celebrate with the two men who had changed her future, her heart and her life.

And the joy that filled her at that thought was as complete as her heart when she was with them.

ALSO BY JESS MICHAELS

The Broken Duke

The Silent Duke

The Duke of Nothing

The Undercover Duke

The Duke of Hearts

The Duke Who Lied

The Duke of Desire

The Last Duke

The Scandal Sheet

The Return of Lady Jane

Stealing the Duke

Lady No Says Yes

My Fair Viscount

Guarding the Countess

The House of Pleasure

Seasons

An Affair in Winter

A Spring Deception

One Summer of Surrender

Adored in Autumn

The Wicked Woodleys

Forbidden

Deceived

Tempted

Ruined

Seduced

Fascinated

To see a complete listing of Jess Michaels' titles, please visit:

http://www.authorjessmichaels.com/books

ABOUT THE AUTHOR

USA Today Bestselling author Jess Michaels likes geeky stuff, Vanilla Coke Zero, anything coconut, cheese and her dog, Elton. She is lucky enough to be married to her favorite person in the world and lives in Oregon settled between the ocean and the mountains.

When she's not obsessively checking her steps on Fitbit or trying out new flavors of Greek yogurt, she writes historical romances with smoking hot characters and emotional stories. She has written for numerous publishers and is now fully indie and loving every moment of it (well, almost every moment).

Jess loves to hear from fans! So please feel free to contact her at Jess@AuthorJessMichaels.com.

Jess Michaels offers a free book to members of her newsletter, so sign up on her website:
http://www.AuthorJessMichaels.com/

[f] facebook.com/JessMichaelsBks
[o] instagram.com/JessMichaelsBks
[BB] bookbub.com/authors/jess-michaels

Made in the USA
Middletown, DE
07 March 2023